Prologue

"Who will live your life?"

The teacher held up a book at the front of the classroom to her pupils. She did not expect a reply, but remained silent to let them think about it for a while. When she was sure that the inquisitive minds in front of her were ready for an explanation she continued.

"That is one of the most important questions you will ever ask yourself. It is also the title of this novel." She tapped the book with her finger. "It doesn't matter if you don't know the answer yet. That's the point. This novel will, hopefully, help you to answer that question."

The teacher started to pace slowly amongst the desks with the book still in her hand. The pupils followed her with their eyes as she continued speaking. "It is likely that some of you are living less than happy lives. By that I mean you might be experiencing events at home that are difficult, painful or distressing. This might be because your parents have broken up or are in the process of breaking up. There could be alcohol, drug or gambling problems in the home. Maybe there are mental health issues. A dysfunctional family life can be caused by a number of factors."

Some of the pupils lowered their gaze and looked uncomfortable, but the teacher carried on. "If you are experiencing any of these things at home it might make you angry, disrespectful, or unwilling or unable to socialise with others. So, those of you who have a happy home life could be affected by someone else's unhappy home life. This could be through confrontation, interruptions during lessons or any number of awkward social interactions. People who are experiencing family issues should be viewed with understanding, even if you are affected negatively by them. You should remember that they were a victim before you became their victim.

"This book will give you an insight to what people with problems at home are going through. Hopefully, this will help you to show empathy towards them when it is needed most. More importantly, if you have a troubled home life it will help you to understand the issues you are dealing with. It will explain how an unhappy family life can affect you while you're growing up, or might affect you in later life. Crucially, it will teach you how to take steps to protect yourself."

The teacher had now made her way around the classroom and was, once again, standing at the front. There was a pile of books on her desk and she put her copy on the top. She sat down to summarise the upcoming lesson.

"You will each be given a copy of the book and we'll take it in turns to read aloud, but it's fine if some of you would prefer not to. At certain points I'll ask you to write down your thoughts about the story and how you feel about it. At the end, we'll dedicate an entire lesson to talking about the book and you can share your feelings but, again, only if you want to.

"So, 'who will live your life?' Only you can decide. Whether you think there is a right or wrong answer is also up to you. The only thing for certain is that the way you live from now on, and the choices you make, will affect your answer." Her last words were spoken in an enquiring voice. "Who will live your life?"

Chapter 1

The classroom emptied into the corridor and the pupils made their way off in various directions. Some left in groups, whereas others walked alone. It was not long before only four of them remained.

Leanne, Oliver, Vincent and Emma stood facing each other in a tight group. Although none of them were very upright in their posture they seemed slightly more content than those who had just sullenly shuffled past them. The end of the school day brought at least some satisfaction.

Oliver was the first to speak. "Hey, Em, how did your physics test go?"

Emma did her best to hide a self-satisfied smile. "I got an A. I ask my teacher if he would mark it straight after I had finished because I had studied so hard for it."

"Teacher's pet!" Leanne said with a smile.

They all chuckled. As close friends, they regularly aimed playful insults at each other.

Vincent rotated his right shoulder and rubbed it awkwardly with this left hand. "I did the shot put today."

Emma knew what the answer would be, but asked anyway. "How did you get on?"

"I came first," Vincent replied casually. "Probably could've thrown further with a few more tries."

Oliver looked at his friend and grinned cheekily. "I always thought these muscles were fake." He squeezed Vincent's bicep.

This brought about another round of laughs. They were comfortable in each other's company and the humorous mocking of each other was never frowned upon. In fact, they valued such interaction.

Emma's next question was aimed at all of them. "Are any of you taking the English oral exam next week?"

Vincent and Oliver shook their heads. "I am," said Leanne. She seemed upbeat about her prospects. "I'm going to pretend that the other people aren't there. That way, I only have to impress myself."

Oliver nodded. "That's a good way of looking at it. Too many people are bothered about what others think." Then he frowned. "Saying that, though, I didn't get an A, win at shot put or prepare for an oral exam today. In fact, I pretty much did nothing of value."

Vincent was not about to accept Oliver's account of his day. "Yeah, right! I saw you give money to that homeless guy at lunch time." He prodded him with his finger accusingly. "And I know that was all the loose change you had."

Leanne put her arm around Oliver. "You're the most caring person I know, Ollie." She kissed him on the cheek. "And you always will be."

The four of them stood smiling until Vincent made a proposal.

"Do you fancy going to the park later?"

Leanne and Oliver nodded, but Emma had other immediate plans.

"Yeah, but I've got to go home and eat first."

"How about six o'clock then?"

"Yeah."

"Yup."

"OK."

At that, they moved off leaving the corridor empty.

The road was long, with green fields on either side. It led away from the outskirts of the town, deep into the countryside. As it got further from the sounds of urban life the stillness of the rural surroundings took over. All became tranquil and time seemed to slow down.

The four teenagers chatted as they made their way along the road. Oliver and Emma walked in front, while Leanne and Vincent followed close behind. Although they had all been close friends from a young age, individually they could not have been more dissimilar. Life had, by chance, thrown them together and they had become best friends.

It was purely down to location that the four of their lives had become intertwined. A little under two decades ago, a private development venture had seen ten houses built on a plot of land well away from the town. They had all been sold within weeks of completion and the acquiring families had soon moved in. Three average size bungalows, seven detached houses, and one very large property, made up the cul-de-sac that was Sanctuary Green. There was even a small area of grassland in the middle to justify its name.

It was luck that the four youngsters were all the same age. Although their brothers and sisters were either older or younger, the four were all in the same year at school. They had formed a close-knit friendship from an early age.

As the four friends approached the cul-de-sac they said their goodbyes and split up to go to their respective homes. It was not long before Sanctuary Green was quiet and peaceful once more. However, within four of the residences, a more unpleasant story was to be told.

As the front door opened the quietness of the street outside was replaced by the sound of a plate hitting a wall. Shouting filled every corner of the house. There was no escaping the sound of raised voices as the two adults went at one another. The relentless barrage of anger and ill-feeling was as unforgiving as it was unrelenting.

Leanne had only just walked through the door when the noise hit her. She stood in the hall with her school bag hanging over her shoulder and a glum look on her face. This was not what she wanted to come home to.

Just coming up to her mid-teens, Leanne had her whole life ahead of her. She was a positive girl, unbothered about her appearance. It was of no concern to her that she was not as slim as other girls her age, and she was happy to wear clothes that were not the latest fashion. She had dressed how she liked from a young age and was not influenced by others. With her unruly hair and slightly spotty complexion, she would never be a catwalk model, but she didn't want to be one anyway. Her beauty was within and that outshone what was on the outside.

Leanne was an independent girl and rarely felt the need for validation from others. She always spoke her mind to her peers, as long as it did not hurt someone else's feelings, and did not pay too much attention to what others thought of her. Not that anyone would have a negative opinion of her anyway, but she was not concerned with people who were critical of her appearance or the way she dressed. Unfortunately, the two people who should have been caring about her were doing very little of that at the current time.

Leanne's parents were having a blistering argument. Paul and Sarah had not been getting on for some time and their differences constantly came to the fore. Such quarrels were becoming more frequent and more aggressive in their nature. The poisonous anger that filled the air was more noxious than the insults that they were yelling at each other. Even though both adults were aiming their barbed abuse at each other, their words were doing damage to the innocent bystander.

"You're useless!"

"Look who's talking!"

"You only had to do one thing."

"Well, why didn't you do it?"

"I was busy."

"So was I."

"You can't even be bothered to get a pair of shoes for your own daughter!"

"It's your turn to pay!"

Now that hurt. That really hurt. The razor blades embedded in the words cut deep into Leanne's flesh. Of all of the things they argued about this was the worst. The focus of this particular clash was her.

Leanne's school bag hit the wooden floor, followed by a tear. The pain she felt inside was not visible to the human eye. If it had been, then maybe her parents would put an end to their conflict. As she made her way towards the stairs to escape to her bedroom, her parents walked into the hall to carry on with their skirmish.

"Just look at her shoes!" Sarah pointed a rigid finger at Leanne's footwear. "They've got scuffs all over them. Don't you care how your daughter looks?"

"You're pointing at a pair of shoes that I paid for." Paul was not about to back down. "How about you make an effort to get some for her? You are her parent as well, you know!"

From this point on the savage words merged into one continual column of noise. Both voices drowned each other out. Words were indistinguishable.

Leanne continued sullenly, moving between them, almost in slow motion. It was a short distance, but a long, agonising journey. There was an angry, snarling face to the left of her and a bellowing, berating voice to the right. She was caught in the crossfire; collateral damage. Not that those firing the shots realised who their stray bullets were hitting.

Leanne reached the stairs and made her way up them, leaving the battle scene behind her. The only evidence of her having been there was her abandoned school bag and a damp patch where her tears had fallen. There was no sign of regret from those who had caused the harm and heartache to her. She was a forgotten casualty of war.

There is no battlefield as destructive as that of the family home. Minds are damaged, souls are shell shocked and the love of life is lost. No side ever truly gains a victory and if someone surrenders, this is rarely answered with an act of mercy. Wars within families are by far the most brutal, unforgiving and catastrophic fought between humans.

Leanne sat on her bed, feeling isolated and unnoticed. She felt so much pain, but had no one to comfort her. The two people who should have been there to console her at this time of sadness were the ones who had caused the anguish. There were so many questions swirling around in her head, yet there was no one to help her answer any of them.

Is it my fault they are arguing?

Maybe I should tell them I would rather keep my old shoes?

Do they know how much I hate it when they fight?

None of these questions were about to be answered by anyone, anytime soon.

Paul and Sarah had been married for two and a half decades. They met a few years before tying the knot and fell in love within a short space of time. As far as most people knew, their marriage had been long and successful. Smiles, hugs and kisses outside of the house gave no indication of the arguments, fights and insult hurling that went on behind closed doors.

Leanne had an older sister, Carrie, but she had left home two years ago. There was a ten year age gap between them, as the elder of the two was an accidental pregnancy and the initial reason for the marriage. Paul and Sarah had wanted to pursue their careers before having another child so waited a decade to have their second. The two daughters were aware of the unintentional factor that had led to the premature start to family life, but that had never caused any conflict.

With both parents enjoying good careers their hard work had paid off. Their house was the largest in Sanctuary Green and they never struggled financially. The fact that they were arguing over who should pay for Leanne's shoes and who should go and buy them was irrelevant. These days they argued about everything. Both of them had the money and the time to get the shoes. This disagreement was simply brought about by a desire to diminish the other and was as good as an excuse as any to start a war of words. So as the sound of conflict filled the house, Leanne remained on her bed, her mind full of torment.

The constant battle in her home life would undoubtedly have an effect on Leanne's future. Sooner or later, she would become the product of the lack of love within the walls of this uncaring home.

Vincent strolled happily along the driveway towards his home. He was a stocky young lad, with a muscular physique. His stature served him well when it came to sport. Football, athletics and most other outdoor activities came to him naturally and he excelled in all of them. As a result, he was usually dressed in sports clothes of some kind.

Vincent had a lively, energetic disposition. His appearance was one of always being ready, willing and able to meet the demands and expectations of physical activity. Whether he was darting around the school corridors, sprinting across the sports field or fidgeting on the spot, he always came across as eager and enthusiastic.

As Vincent opened the front door he saw something that made his heart sink. His expression quickly went from upbeat to downcast. With his shoulders slumped and his head bowed he entered his home and closed the door behind him.

The sight of an empty beer can was an ominous sign. Alcohol at this time of day was never a good thing and invariably led to misery. Consumption would normally start late morning and continue throughout the day. Round about now the consequence of such a large intake of intoxicants would be at its worst.

Vincent hated it when his stepfather drank. The fact that the beer can was lying on the floor in the hall and not in a bin was a sure sign that the alcohol had already taken an effect. Somewhere in the house lurked a drunken individual who would be annoying at best and detestable at worst.

With a frown on his face, Vincent moved tentatively through the house. There was no sign of his stepfather in the living room or the kitchen, although he did find more empty beer cans. He climbed the stairs to check the bedrooms, his footsteps deliberately soft so as not to wake anyone who might be sleeping. However, when he glanced in each of the rooms, he was relieved to find there was no one there.

Vincent made his way back downstairs to prepare himself something to eat. As he entered the kitchen he started to plan his meal. Fruit and vegetables would be the main ingredients of the dish he had in mind. He rolled up his sleeves and began to gather the utensils he required. Then the back door opened.

Jack stood in the doorway for a moment, eying his stepson, and then stumbled inside. He had a beer can in one hand and a cigarette in the other. As he closed the door behind him with a kick of his leg, he sniffed, swallowed whatever was caught in the back of his throat and burped loudly.

The differences between stepfather and stepson could not have been more apparent. Jack's appearance was one of apathy and sloth. His white vest was stained with food and his jeans were covered in greasy blotches. An unkempt quiff hung over his brow and stubble adorned his chin. This was a person who no longer cared about their appearance, who showed no sign of endeavour or success.

As Jack spoke to his stepson he shook the empty can in his hand. "Get me a beer!"

Vincent gestured with his hand. "You're closer to the fridge than I am."

Jack did not like being disobeyed and threw his empty beer can at his stepson. It missed. Nevertheless, he repeated his demand in a more aggressive tone. "Get me a beer, now!"

Although Vincent had a better physique than his stepfather, Jack was a good twenty years older than him and had more strength due to years of manual labour. This gave him the upper hand when it came to confrontations like this, and they both knew it.

Reluctantly, Vincent walked over to the fridge and pulled out a beer. Jack took two steps towards his stepson. He now stood within inches of him. His stare was cold and menacing, and his shoulders were pulled back as if he was about to strike. He grabbed the beer out of Vince's hands. Vincent knew it was time to leave. The utensils for making his meal were laid out on the kitchen table, but he knew better than to stick around. He turned to walk away, but it was too late.

Jack took the cigarette from his non-drinking hand and put it in his mouth. With a swipe of his palm he cracked Vincent around the back of his head. There was no retaliation. His stepson staggered unsteadily out of the kitchen and out of harm's way. At least that was his hope.

Keen to reinforce his alpha-male status, Jack followed his stepson. They were now in the hall, which was narrow and confined, with little space to avoid incoming blows. Jack kicked Vincent in the back of his thigh. His stepson turned towards him, but no words were spoken. Another kick was delivered to the calf. Still nothing was said.

Vincent had flinched at both blows, but had not reacted further. He knew better than to remonstrate. Years of such violent encounters had taught him to passively endure the onslaught and not retaliate. It was like waiting for a storm to blow itself out.

There were times in the past when Vincent had sworn at his stepfather or pushed him away when on the receiving end of such unnecessary chastisement. This had always resulted in a significantly worse beating. So now, he stood there with his head bowed, not saying a word.

Jack had been drinking heavily all day and was not about to overexert himself. He gave his stepson one last kick and made his way back to the kitchen to finish his beer. There was no explanation for what he had just done and there certainly was no attempt to justify it, not that he could if he tried. It had all been a display of aggression to make sure that he was acknowledged as the man of the house.

The fact that Vincent had, at first, refused to get a beer for his stepfather was irrelevant. Even if he had done so straight away, Jack would have found another reason to lash out. He had been unemployed for the last two months and the pressure of not being able to pay the bills and provide for his family was starting to have an effect on him. Such inadequacies made him feel like he was losing his manliness. The only way to alleviate this feeling was to stamp down someone close to him, to raise his own stature.

Vincent closed his bedroom door behind him and slumped down on to his bed. He rubbed the back of his legs and winced at the throbbing pain. It hurt more on the inside though. The mental agony was far worse.

If his mother, Fiona, had been there it might have been different. Sometimes she could control Jack, but other times she would provoke an even worse reaction resulting in her also suffering maltreatment at the hands of her husband. Love did not stand in the way of anger and abuse. In fact, those who were closest made the most favourable targets.

Jack and Fiona had been married for a little over four years. They had been together for twice as long as that. A baby daughter, Jade, was added to the family in the last nine months. The violence had started in the winter that followed.

Loans taken out, unemployment due to the recession and alcohol had all contributed towards the change in Jack. With the misguided view that his wife and stepson thought little of him because of his enforced shortcomings, his only response was to hurt those closest to him. He deluded himself that his behaviour solidified his position as head of the household. He failed to realise that this change of character had the opposite effect. Neither of his victims looked up to him, they simply feared him.

Vincent's biological father had left his mother two years after he was born. He had seen photos of him, but had never met him. There was no immediate desire to seek contact with him either. In his view you can't miss something you have never had.

With his mother out of the house collecting his younger sister from nursery, Vincent had no one to turn to. Sitting in his room in a state of physical and mental pain, he had to suffer alone and in silence. There was sadness and anger, as well as confusion and torment. That is how it had been for years now and would probably be for more to come.

The violence that Vincent suffered at the hands of his stepfather would inevitably affect him later in life. Sooner or later his suppressed feelings would have to be expelled, and those around him would undoubtedly suffer. It was like he was a ticking time bomb, waiting to explode.

The silence in the house was broken as the front door slowly swung open. A set of keys dropped to the hall floor and sent an echo throughout. After the door closed, all that could be heard was the breathing of the person who stood there alone and unmoving.

Emma was used to coming home from school and not receiving a welcome. Solitude was a frequent companion within the walls of this lifeless dwelling. All she had to keep her company was her own thoughts. However, her mind was not producing many of those right now.

As Emma slowly walked towards the kitchen she pulled a piece of paper out of her school bag. It was the physics test she had taken earlier that day. She took a magnet out of a small pot and attached the completed exam sheet to the fridge door. There was a large 'A', written in red ink, at the top. At no point would she receive any word of congratulations or expressions of pride from her mother, and none were expected.

On the kitchen table, Emma found the usual note and picked it up. She gave it a quick glance before putting it down again. It simply informed her that her dinner was in the usual place; the oven, so she turned it on to 200°c. There was no one home to do it for her and certainly no one about to share the meal with.

While waiting for her food to cook, Emma stood in the kitchen gazing at the back of her hands. She then turned them over so she could see her palms. After a short while she twisted her wrists again to show her knuckles.

Emma was a tall, thin girl, with short hair and a slender frame. There was little shape to her body and she often wondered if she was 'too skinny'. This was hardly surprising considering she invariably had to prepare her own meals and could not always be bothered.

Those who knew Emma were aware of her quiet and withdrawn nature. She had little to say, but at the same time she would never be impolite or ignore someone. Her silent demeanour had nothing to do with shyness, in fact, when she was with her closest friends she talked as much as any of them. She preferred to listen rather than speak. It was a more efficient way to learn.

Emma was in the top set for all subjects and passed every test that she sat. This was not only due to her being of above average intelligence, but also because she was willing to put in the hours of work required. Her studiousness was matched only by her enthusiasm to apply herself to each of her subjects. Her efforts were regularly rewarded with an A grade at school, but unfortunately this was not usually recognised at home.

Emma's mother, Karen, was rarely around to praise her daughter. She had little option. Her jobs at the call centre and local bars took up too much time. If she had the choice she would have been at home and proud of every 'A', but as a single mum, solely responsible for the rent and bills, it was just not possible.

Michael and Ellie, Emma's brother and sister, had both moved out in recent years. They had found jobs and left home to make their own lives. Everyone was pleased for them, even though it made life more economically challenging for their mother. As a loving parent, Karen was pleased to see them start their lives and enjoy their freedom, even if she did miss them terribly.

As for Emma's father, Carl, that was a sad story for all of them. When he and Karen married, they truly meant their vows; 'til death do us part'. They were deeply in love and their family meant everything to them. Sadly, after contracting cancer in his early thirties, he died, leaving behind three young children and a widow. Fate had acted cruelly and left a huge chasm their lives.

So, with her mother working long hours, her father long passed and her siblings living their own lives, Emma regularly found herself alone in an empty house, with her own thoughts. This was her struggle. Not the loneliness or lack of attention, but the confines of her mind.

Emma stood in the kitchen and gazed idly around. Her attention eventually came to centre on her hands as she pressed them down on the table in front of her. As she spread her fingers, she saw triangles and she tried to make them all the same size. When she put her palms together she attempted to make the shape symmetrical. This was not optional, but essential. It was vital to bring order to disorder and her obsession to do so was compulsive.

Every ornament must be lined up exactly. All numbers must be multiplied, divided, added and subtracted so that they could relate to the number seven. Patterns must be made symmetrical and counted. This was crucial for her to function properly, even though none of it made sense. She would like not to have to do it, but her mind was not hers to control.

Emma had not been diagnosed with a mental disorder, because she had not spoken to anyone about her problems. She had never been given the chance. If her mother had realised her daughter had mental health issues, she would have tried to help her. However, a person can only solve a problem when they realise there is one.

At no point in her life had Emma become aware that she had psychological difficulties. She had grown up thinking the way her mind worked was normal. Seeing patterns, counting numbers and the compulsive desire to put objects in a neat order were regular obsessions that she found herself contending with. Whether it was seeing shapes on repeating wallpaper, counting the windows on a building or arranging the ornaments on a window sill, she felt a habitual urge to complete the unnecessary, illogical tasks she set herself.

There were times when Emma could go for long periods of almost up to a week without creating a compulsion that would have to be obsessively acted upon, but there were also days when they became severe. This was one such moment. The shapes, patterns and numbers were attacking her mind like a well-organised army. A barrage of triangles, symmetry and numeric values probed her thoughts, wave after wave. It was a battle that her consciousness was losing.

Emma knew that there was no logic to what was going on inside her head. It was not important that the shapes were the same size or that her left hand was an exact mirror image of her right. There was certainly no need for the numbers to add up to seven. However, at times like this her mind gave her no choice but to try to bring order to disorder, even though it only led to further disarray. This was never meant to make sense. If there was an instant cure that would clear her head of these meaningless mechanisms she would have grasped it willingly, but it seemed a remedy was not available to her.

In an attempt to alleviate the turmoil in her mind, Emma decided to cut up some cheese to put on her lasagne that was now cooking in the oven. She got a block of cheddar out of the fridge and pulled a knife from the holder on the work top. This was the worst thing that she could have done at this moment. Cutting shapes while such a relentless battle was being fought in her mind did not bode well.

As Emma rested the sharp knife on the cheese she had several goes at straightening the blade so it was exactly parallel to the edge of the block. With a downward motion she sliced a segment away. It was not perfect though. Her attempt was a few millimetres out at the bottom due to the slanted angle at which she had cut it.

To make up for her failed first effort, Emma quickly sliced off another segment. This was also not exact in its proportion. She hurriedly sliced away a third piece. Once again she was unsuccessful. Realising that she was not achieving her goal she forced herself to stop.

Emma tried to block out the chaos in her mind. She braced herself, clenched her fists and rested her knuckles on the cutting block. Closing her eyes, she took a deep breath. She stood unmoving, trying to withstand the attack on her consciousness. It was then that she realised she had done more harm to herself than usual. The knife was imbedded into her left palm. She had unknowingly been clasping at the blade without feeling the pain. Blood had already started to ooze from the wound. Still she did not release her grip. A person can experience two types of suffering; that of the body and that of the mind. Sometimes the brain can cause far more agony than could be inflicted upon the physical being.

As she became more aware of the pain in her hand, Emma felt relieved, for it took over the space in her mind occupied by the compulsive obsessions. Although her skin was hurting badly, the pain seemed to reduce the turmoil in her mind. Only when the blood from her hand started to drip on to the floor did Emma pull out the knife. As she looked at the deep cut to her palm she suddenly realised what she had done, heaping more stress on her already overloaded mind.

Grabbing a handful of kitchen roll, Emma applied it to the wound, shaking her head in disbelief at her own actions. It had only made things worse; her pain had simply doubled. Although it felt for a moment that she had alleviated her suffering, it short lived. Even as she stood there berating herself for what she had done, she couldn't help noticing that the knife was not symmetrical to the edge of the work top.

It would not be the last time Emma would do something to cause her harm. Her mental health issues, coupled with the fact she was unaware she had them, meant the future did not look bright for Emma. With no one to help her to cope with these problems, sooner or later, they would only get worse.

"Hi, Oliver."

"Hi, Mum."

The greeting was cordial and pleasant. It was how a mother and son should welcome each other. There was evidently warmth to their relationship and the two of them made no attempt to hide their affection for each other. Even though they were standing in the front garden, in full public view, mother and son were willing to let the world see how much they felt for each other. A hug and kiss on her cheek confirmed their mutual devotion.

As Oliver made his way into the house he left his mother watering the front garden. As he entered the hall he came across his father. Their greeting was similarly pleasant.

"Hi, Dad."

"Hello, Oliver."

There was no hugging or kissing, and the pair continued on their way to do whatever task they had set themselves.

As Oliver made his way into the living room he picked up the remote and switched on the TV. There was nothing in particular that he wanted to watch, but he flicked through the channels anyway. None of the programmes interested him much and it was only when he came across a children's activity show, with assault courses, that he kept it on simply because he was bored with pressing the same button over and over.

Oliver was a short lad, with a slight build. His hands, feet and facial features were all small, but they were not out of proportion to the rest of his body. Being so diminutive, he looked younger than he actually was. In fact, he would regularly be mistaken for a child rather than an adolescent.

Although small in stature, Oliver made up for it with his lively personality. He was never one to be quiet and withdrawn and was happy to be the centre of attention. For someone so physically inconspicuous people were always aware of his presence in the room.

While Oliver was disinterestedly watching the children on television, climbing up a rope ladder, his mother stepped into the living room and put her gardening gloves on the sideboard.

"I've got to go out shopping. The roses need some plant food because of the dry weather." She smiled wryly. "If you want you can mow the lawn."

"I'll give it a miss, thanks." Oliver grinned back at her and motioned towards the television. "Even daytime TV is more appealing than that."

Jean had expected that response from her son. She did not blame him for his apathy. She was not a keen gardener and only kept up the appearance of the front of the house because the neighbours made such an effort with theirs. It was not because she felt pressured into it, but she did not want the front garden to spoil Sanctuary Green by becoming overgrown and full of weeds.

Like her son, Jean was also of small stature. Her body was so petite it was hard to imagine that she had, at one point in her life, given birth to her only child. However, this did not hold her back when it came to her appearance. She was always well-dressed and her hair was regularly crafted into a new style. Even though she carried the diminutive family genes her glowing demeanour made her stand out.

As Jean pulled her car keys out of her pocket she turned away and spoke without looking back. "As your father has just got back from a business trip, he'd probably like to spend some time with you." She waved her hand as she left, calling out, "I won't be long."

Oliver did not reply. He had already seen his father and had no wish to spend more time with him. It was not because he did not love his dad; he cared for him like any son would, he just didn't want to be alone in his company. In fact, quite the opposite.

Oliver thought for a moment before turning off the television and throwing the remote control back on the coffee table. With a quick glance around he headed upstairs to get changed into more comfy clothes. As he reached the landing he could see that his bedroom door was open. This was not how he left it.

Before Oliver could change direction and run back down the stairs his father, Brian appeared in the doorway.

"Going out already?" he said, stepping forward on to the landing. "I've only just got back. It's been two weeks since we last saw each other."

Oliver was only too aware of this; he had counted every day. It had been a relief when his dad was away and he had secretly been dreading his return.

Just then, the sound of Jean's car could be heard pulling off the driveway. Father and son were both aware of it. It did not need drawing attention to, but Brian did anyway.

"Your mother's going out." He rubbed his chin. "Did she say how long she'd be?"

"A few minutes," Oliver said. He had no idea, but made up a lie regardless. "She's going to the shop and will be right back."

Brian inched closer. Oliver shuffled backwards uncomfortably, even though he was near the top of the stairs.

"It's OK. I don't bite," Brian said, in an attempt to calm his son. He feigned a laugh. "I am your dad, you know."

Brian was slightly taller than Oliver, but he was still below average build. He was not physically imposing, but he had a presence about him that made it known he was in control. His clothes were always neatly ironed and it was obvious that they had cost a lot of money. His shoes were shiny and, if he wore a suit, his tie would remain neatly in place at all times. The only two things about his appearance that seemed slightly out of place were his colourful glasses and his long hair that was tied back into a ponytail, as if to show that he had a fun and relaxed side.

Although Brian's appearance gave the impression that he was self-disciplined, it was just a facade. In fact, as he leered at his son, he was clearly not even trying to restrain his instincts. His emotionless eyes were empty, as if he had switched off his human side.

Oliver stood facing his father, with his gaze lowered, in a deflated posture. He closed his eyes, and a tear rolled down his cheek at the thought of what was about to come.

Brian said, "Relax."

At that, the father put his hand where no man should touch his son. This was an act so evil that there can never be any justification for it. When someone commits murder they may have a reason why they did it. If someone is killed their body is dead, whereas with this atrocious crime the life is taken away from the victim, but they still have to endure the suffering.

Although the sickly contact had only lasted for a few seconds, Oliver could not take anymore. He reeled away and put his hands up in a defensive manner to say 'enough'.

"I've got to go to the toilet," he said, taking a tentative step towards the bathroom. "I really need to go." The real reason to why he had pulled away was obvious, but he made up a lie, nonetheless.

"Really?" Brian said casually, trying to defuse the awkwardness of the situation. "If you've got to go, you'd better go."

At that, Oliver ran quickly to the toilet and locked the door behind him. A cold silence filled the house. Nothing stirred and time seemed to stop.

Oliver stood with his back pressed up against the toilet door, while Brian lurked at the top of the stairs with a half-smile on his face. One of them was experiencing extreme emotional turmoil, while the other was elated. Their feelings could not have been more polarised.

Brian could not control himself because he did not want to. His lack of self-control was deliberate. It is every father's instinct to protect their children, but Brian appeared to be able to ignore this part of himself. He selfishly let his sick desires rule him and he certainly never suffered any guilt for his actions.

The abuse had been going on since Oliver was an infant. No one knew about it, of course. At first, Brian had told his son that it was their secret. A child's naivety is easily exploited.

As Oliver got older it became obvious to Brian that his son was beginning to work out that it was very wrong, so he told him that it would rip the family apart if he ever told anyone. Brian regularly stressed how much it would destroy Jean if they had to be separated from each other. In an act of self-serving deception, he told his son that he would be the one to blame if their lives were ruined.

Now that Oliver was well into his teens it did not happen as often as it used to. The sickening episodes normally only occurred when his father had been away for a long time on business. It was as if the evil thoughts built up in his mind and he then dished them out when they became too big to ignore.

Although Oliver was increasingly able to walk away, the option of pushing back was not a viable one for someone as physically ill-equipped for confrontation as he was. As much as he was outspoken and energetic, he was simply not a fighter. There had been times when he had quietly asked his father not to do what he was doing, but this normally had no effect whatsoever. The lack of consent actually seemed to add to the enjoyment.

After about five minutes, Brian realised that his moment of self-gratification was over, so he made his way downstairs. He did not care that he had left nothing but torment in his wake, but he never did. At the top of his agenda were his own selfish, disgusting desires. As for his son, he would have to suffer silently and accept the situation.

Satisfied that the painful, grievous episode was over, Oliver hurriedly undressed to get in the shower. As he got under the water he scrubbed himself in a fruitless attempt to cleanse himself of the dirtiness. The more he scoured his flesh the more his skin became red raw. No matter how hard he tried he could not purge the feelings of revulsion.

It was clear that this would affect Oliver for the rest of his life. There would be no question of the damage done to him, but whether it would influence his interaction with others was yet to be seen. He had a long, arduous road ahead of him with no one to help. With such terrible anguish tearing at his mind it seemed as though one more broken soul would be sent out into society with potentially grave consequences.

Oliver, Vincent and Emma were all in their respective bedrooms thinking about what they had just been through. Each of them had headphones on, isolating them from the world around them. They were all streaming the same live music channel and the lyrics to the track that was currently playing seemed to sum up what they were going through; 'All You Need Is Love' by the Beatles, was being covered by one of the latest artists who was big in the charts. The words said it all. They did need love. It was quite simply all they needed.

Tears flowed, anger built, despair flourished, and pain tormented all four friends. With no one to turn to, each of them had to cope with their problems on their own. They were forced to endure hurt-filled lives with no help and no one to rely on. No one knew about their suffering, but them.

A soft breeze blew across the park making the grass dance to its tune. The trees and flower beds added a colourful palette to the scenery, painting a picture of serenity and harmony. The sun shone, bathing those below in pleasant warm glow. Unfortunately, the four souls at the centre of this celestial canvas were not so restful.

Leanne, Oliver, Vincent and Emma lay on their backs on the grass, staring up at the sky. Each of them had their heads close to each other so that their bodies formed a cross when viewed from above. When they visited the park they would often lie like this. It meant they could all be close to each other, but allow their minds to wonder as they talked. They were there, but not completely.

With all that had gone on earlier in their homes none of them was in the mood for chatting. If anyone looked closely enough they might just see the signs of what they had each been through. Emma had a large cut on her hand, which was now bandaged up, whereas Vincent had a bruise to his leg, concealed by his jeans. Oliver was red and sore all over, and Leanne had puffy eyes. They each had scars from the battlefield.

It was a long time before any of them spoke. Vincent finally broke the silence. "I was glad to get out of the house." He rubbed the side of his leg. "It gets so stuffy inside at this time of year."

Leanne nodded in agreement. "I know. I couldn't wait to get out." She blinked repeatedly to ease her irritated, red eyes. "It's too crowded at my place sometimes. I know it's just my parents and me, but everyone gets in each other's way."

"You should try living at my place," said Emma, with a frown on her face. "There's never anyone there."

"It must be nice though. Being alone and having our own space."

"That depends." Emma was not so sure.

"On what?" Vincent asked.

"On who you have to keep you company." Emma raised her hand and pointed her finger downwards circling it round her friends. "I'd rather spend time with you guys than be at home on my own."

Leanne raised her hand and clasped hold of Emma's in a show of solidarity. "Same here."

The other two lifted their arms as well and they all grabbed hold of each other's hands. As a group they always supported each other and would never leave anyone out. If one of them took a fall, the others would all be there to pick them up.

Up until this point, Oliver hadn't said a word, but now he joined in. "I'd much rather be with all of you, too." He took a moment to think about what he was going to say next. "You're like my family anyway."

Although they all agreed with this sentiment, none of them realised the significance. Not even Oliver was aware of the gravity of what he had just said. These four unhappy adolescents had never caused any harm to one another, the source of all their unhappiness came from their families. Whether through oblivious neglect or deliberate harm, their sorrows originated at home. Oliver's remark was untrue. They were nothing like his family.

Considering how close they all were, talking to each other about what they were going through might have been the best course of action, but it was just not an option. It would have been extremely uncomfortable for them to talk to each other about the things that were happening at home. How do you explain how much it hurts when your parents argue all the time or tell your friends you are the victim of violence? Mental health issues were really difficult to explain to someone anyway, and as for sexual abuse, people would not even want to start a conversation about that. They all felt they could not speak to anyone about what they were going through, not even each other, even though they all trusted each other completely.

Emma started a new topic. "What do you think about that book we're reading at school?"

"You mean the one about people who have dysfunctional home lives?" Oliver replied.

"Yeah." Emma sounded contemplative. "The teacher said it helps understand that sort of thing."

"Apparently it's about how to deal with it too." A curious expression crossed Leanne's face. "Do you reckon it would help someone in that situation?"

Vincent took a moment to think about it and then did his best to answer. "It probably would. It certainly couldn't do any harm." He sounded almost optimistic. "Anything is worth a go, if things are that bad."

"Sometimes when people are going through something that terrible any bit of help can make a difference." Oliver said wistfully. "Why wouldn't someone give it a try?"

"What was the book called again?" Leanne asked.

"Who will live your life?"

Chapter 2

"Quiet please!" The teacher said in a decisive, yet pleasant voice. "I want to get the lesson underway."

It did not take long for the pupils to stop talking and settle down. They had a lot of admiration for this particular teacher and always did as she asked. The fear of being punished was rarely a factor. She had earned their respect through years of good tutoring and doing her best for them.

Mrs Reason was liked throughout the school. She was a skilled professional, willing to give up her time for whoever needed it. Her advice was readily available and always valuable. These positive attributes and her excellent reputation meant that she was popular with her students and fellow teachers alike.

Mrs Reason was a dwarf. Standing at just over four foot tall, she was diminutive. She appeared tallest when sat at her desk. When she walked amongst the pupils in the classroom she could not see over them and all they could see was the top of her head. None of this mattered though, as she was more than able to command her students' attention. This was evident as she began the lesson.

"At no point in your life will you be surrounded by so many people who want the best for you as you are at this moment in time. Teachers, such as I, do not do this job for money, especially as we get paid so little. We do it because we care. There is not one of us who has not spent years training to be a teacher and who doesn't have a passion for the profession. We know what's best for you and we want what's best for you." A hopeful look came over her face. "In the future I want every one of you to have a good life. I want you to have a job you enjoy, a nice family and to be healthy of body and mind. If, at some point, I bump into any of you after you've left school I really hope that you can tell me you are doing well for yourself. That is why I'm here."

The pupils listened carefully to every word Mrs Reason said. None of them doubted her sincerity and they were willing to put their futures in her capable hands. She had their full respect.

Mrs Reason got up off her chair and picked up a book on her desk. "Now that we've started reading this book some of you might associate yourself with one or more of the characters. You might have parents who argue, parents who don't spend much time at home, parents who hurt you or..." She paused and a serious expression came over her face. "You might have parents who do worse than that."

Some of the pupils in the classroom felt uncomfortable at this point; four of them in particular. A few bowed their heads, whereas others shifted uncomfortably in their chairs. Others sat rigidly, trying to not to show that they felt awkward. It was understandable that they did not want their feelings known, and Mrs Reason knew this, which is why she now spoke to the ones who were not experiencing any distress.

"Those of you who do not relate directly to any of the characters in the book probably know someone who is like them. Maybe you have a friend whose parents don't have much money so they both have to work very long hours and are not around the home much. You might have been to someone's house when there have been arguments, or you might have seen a member of their family drunk or abusing drugs." She raised the book above her head. "I doubt there is anyone in this classroom who doesn't know someone whose life is in some way similar to one of the characters in this novel. Such dysfunctional home lives are commonplace these days."

Once Mrs Reason had made sure everyone in the class could relate to the lesson she went about describing its relevance to them. "What I'm trying to say is that this book affects all of you. That boy you know whose parents are going through a divorce might be short-tempered towards those around him. The girl who you sit next to, who makes you feel uncomfortable, might be struggling with mental health problems. There are a number of ways people with dysfunctional family lives can affect you."

Mrs Reason bowed her head and took a deep breath. "And that brings me on to the extremely awkward subject I know a lot of you are already finding uncomfortable; sexual abuse. It's a topic no one wants to read about, or talk about, but imagine for a moment how the victim of a paedophile feels. Think what it must be like to live with a secret like that. This book does not just highlight the more common causes of a dysfunctional home life, such as domestic violence, drugs and mental health issues, but also the most extreme. You never know what the person next to you might be going through. So you need to be brave and willing to tackle this awful subject. Let's make sure we leave no one behind."

Some of the pupils watched Mrs Reason as she began walking amongst the desks, whereas others lowered their gaze so they could concentrate on what she was saying. Either way, every one of them took her words on board and realised how important it was for each of them individually to be a part of the lesson.

"Before we move on," she continued. "You've got to realise something that is fundamental to the heart of this lesson. This is the most significant thing that you are going to learn." She looked around the class and raised her voice to emphasise the importance of her words. "The opposite of love is hate. If someone is not receiving enough love then they will give out hate. This can manifest in two ways: they either hate themselves or they hate others."

Mrs Reason could see that what she was trying to explain was difficult for some of the pupils to understand. "I'll give you an example. Imagine you're at a party with three of your friends. A guy comes along and introduces themselves to your group. He shakes hands or hugs each of your pals. They immediately take a liking to him as he seems really likeable and fun. This person wins your friends over as he cracks jokes, tells them stories and makes them laugh." She lowered her voice. "However, this really entertaining person completely ignores you. They don't say a word to you. When they're telling their funny jokes and interesting stories they don't even look at you. Their attention is directed towards your friends. They've got no time for you whatsoever. How does this make you feel?"

Mrs Reason knew she was not going to get an answer, so she added, "It makes you feel bad, doesn't it? Even though this guy is clearly charismatic and fun, you can't bring yourself to like him. He's ignored you and made you feel insignificant and worthless. You immediately begin to dislike him. Why?" Once again she was not expecting an answer. "The reason is that he hasn't shown you any warmth, so you haven't warmed to him. You weren't expecting much affection from him, so you don't despise him, but that little bit of affection that you might have felt has turned to dislike. You've received no love, so in return you give hate. That is what happens if a person wants love, but doesn't get any. They end up hating the people they want love from or themselves. The opposite of love is hate."

Mrs Reason stopped talking for a short while so that what she had said could sink in. She walked to the front of the class and sat down, watching her pupils carefully to gauge their reaction. It was as well for her to know which of them was responding well to the lesson and those who were not. Some of them were talking amongst themselves, which was a good sign as it meant they were participating in the assignment. Others were sitting quietly with a distant expression on their face, deep in thought. This was also okay as they were probably coming to their own conclusions on the subject matter.

Mrs Reason carried on with the lesson. "Now that you know what is happening in the lives of the four main characters you will see how it begins to affect them beyond their homes. It's important that you make the connection between the lack of love and attention they are getting, and how they behave as a result." She then raised her copy of the book in the air. "I want you to turn to the page where we left off and I will choose someone to read."

Mrs Reason watched as the pupils opened their books, ready to begin. After a quick glance around the classroom, she picked out a young girl who was sitting at the front and instructed her to read aloud.

Oliver and Leanne were in the school corridor chatting. Neither of them knew the whereabouts of Vincent and Emma, it was just the two of them. It was not unusual for the four friends to fragment and spend time apart, but still be in each other's company. There were never any feelings of jealousy or rejection and they all knew they would be back as a foursome in the near future.

Leanne was leaning against a wall. "Are you going to that party at Tommy Doyle's this Saturday?"

Oliver looked confused. "Party? What Party?"

"God, Ollie, you're so forgetful at times." Leanne laughed and playfully pushed his shoulder with her fingertips. "We were talking about it last weekend. Everyone at school is going on about it. You know, he lives in the big red house, with the huge garden, on the outskirts of town."

A sudden look of realisation crossed Oliver's face. "Ah, yeah, I remember." He made an exaggerated gesture with his arms outstretched to imply magnitude. "The house is as big as his ego."

"Yeah, that's the one." Leanne smiled. "So are you going?"

"It'd be rude not to," Oliver said cheekily. "It wouldn't be any fun without me."

"Well, why do you think I was asking?" Leanne played along, but then looked down at her feet. "I'll have to buy those new shoes at the weekend though."

"What, the red ones from the shopping centre?" Oliver replied.

"Yeah, they're a bit pricey, but I want to feel marvellous." She lifted her right leg and wriggled her foot. "I don't think it will hurt for me to feel marvellous for once."

They suddenly found themselves interrupted.

"Nice legs!"

Leanne wore an expression of contempt on her face as she glanced up to see who had made the remark, but the uninvited speaker had not yet finished.

"No really. Nice legs." The words were spoken with a smile. "Just thought I'd say, you know."

Brad Jacobs: smoother than silk and sharper than splinters. He had a way with words which he used to gain favour. If anyone knew how to charm a girl, it was him. He was like champagne and caviar when all you wanted was coffee and cake.

Brad made a gesture of surrender with his hands. "Hey, I hope you don't mind. It's just a compliment." He motioned towards the target of his admiration. "I like nice things, and your legs are very nice."

Leanne was taken aback by the unexpectedness of it all. One minute she was talking about something as mundane as getting new shoes and then the next she was being complimented on the way she looked. In fact, she was being made to feel good about herself. This was a pleasant feeling and she liked it.

"Well, thanks." She seemed embarrassed by the unexpected attention. "They're just legs though," she said dismissively.

Brad realised that the bait had been taken, so he went about making sure the trap was triggered. "Not that there's anything wrong with the rest of you." The first compliment seemed to have worked, so the next should too. "Your face is nice too."

Leanne blushed and put her fingers to her face in an effort to hide it.

"I know girls who would kill for your cheek bones. They frame those great eyes you have. That's what makes you so attractive." Brad fixed his gaze on his prey. "It's a bit like a painting. All the best works of art need highlighting."

"Well, if I'm a work of art I must be priceless," said Leanne cockily.

"Whoa! You're a feisty one." Brad raised his hands in a submissive manner. "I better watch out for you."

Leanne chuckled and lowered her gaze. It felt good to have someone show her some attention. She was sure Brad was just messing around, but his comments made her feel warm inside. Surely there was no harm in her feeling good about herself for once.

After months of her parents arguing in front of her without them realising how much it was hurting her, Leanne felt elated to actually be noticed. When her mother and father were screaming at each other invariably they were not even aware that she was in the room. This made her feel insignificant and abandoned. Even when she cried they rarely noticed, and if they did they would blame each other for upsetting her, but that just made things worse as Leanne then felt like the argument was her fault.

Brad had appeared and changed things. He had noticed her and acknowledged, and that was all that was needed. It had not taken a lot to win Leanne over, because she was not used to being the recipient of admiration. Someone who constantly receives affection may not be so easily influenced the first time they receive a compliment. If her parents had been more attentive and showed her that they were concerned about her feelings, she would not have been so easily influenced by Brad.

Brad went about securing his prize. "You know, you're alright you are." He already knew the answer to the question he was about to ask, but it was all part of his plan. "What's your name?"

"Leanne." She tried her best to appear cool and unflustered. "And you are?"

That was what Brad wanted to hear. He already knew Leanne's name as he had seen her around the school and asked someone, he simply wanted to find out if she was really interested in him. Her question confirmed his success. "Brad. Brad Jacobs," he said, feigning an expression of respect.

Brad's well-rehearsed routine was going to plan. First bait the trap. He had done that. Then when the prey is caught, make sure it doesn't escape. Leanne was not going anywhere soon. All he had to do was go in for the kill.

"Are you going to Tommy's party this Saturday?" he asked.

"Yes, I am."

"Cool. Then I'll see you there. Be sure to bring those legs with you."

At that the conversation ended.

Leanne giggled and quickly brought her knees together. She was a bit uncomfortable with his advances, but she also felt rather tingly inside. She had felt awkward under Brad's scrutiny, but good at the same time to have been appraised so highly. It was only then she realised that someone was staring at her.

"Oh my God!" Oliver had watched the whole encounter. "I can't believe that just happened."

"I know! I know!" Leanne looked at her friend in excitement, expecting him to give his approval. "Well?"

"Well what?"

"What do you think I should do?"

Oliver paused for a moment, then said in a playful manner. "I think you need to party, girl!"

They laughed and shared a hug.

Then, Leanne turned to face her friend. "What about you Ollie? We've got to set you up with someone too." She raised her eyebrows in a suggestive manner. "I reckon we could find someone hot for you."

This was not what Oliver wanted to hear. Sex was not something he wanted to think about. For him it represented physical and mental pain. Whereas other youngsters of his age were excitedly finding out about it, he had only ever experienced it in a cruel way. It was not something he felt he would enjoy.

Oliver wanted to fit in, naturally, but the topic was, understandably, very uncomfortable for him. Participating in the actual act itself would be even more difficult. However, he could not tell anyone why he wasn't interested, so he had to pretend that he was keen.

"Sounds good to me," he said, feigning interest.

"It shouldn't be too difficult. You're not too bad yourself, Ollie." Leanne teased. She made a sensual gesture with her hands. "I can imagine someone rubbing their hands all over you."

This did not go down well. A shudder rippled through Oliver's body. He swallowed down a feeling of nausea. He did not mind bodily contact, but he had to feel as though he was in control. Whenever his father had touched him it had not been through his own choice.

Oliver tried to force a smile, but it was not convincing. This was getting too uncomfortable, so he tried to dismiss the subject. "I'm not that bothered if I don't get with someone though."

"Why?"

Oliver's smile left his face. "I've got to go to the toilet."

At that, he quickly escaped, leaving Leanne alone in the corridor looking perplexed. She had sensed that something was not right, but had understandably not worked out what it was. With a shake of the head, she shrugged off the incident and got out her phone to pass the time while she waited for her friend to return. She would have a long wait.

Emma and Vincent were huddled together on a bench on the edge of the schoolyard watching people. Neither of them spoke. Pupils of all shapes and sizes walked past them and their gaze went to each one in turn.

The elements were having an effect on the passers-by. Coats fluttered, hair ruffled and groups of pupils clustered together to protect themselves from the unforgiving gale. Leaves and the occasional food wrapper whistled past those who braved the conditions, to the point that the majority of them would be glad when the break was over. Getting back to their lessons was not normally a welcome prospect, but today the warmness of the classroom would be well received.

As the wind brushed against Emma's legs she noticed a leaflet wrapped around her ankle. She bent down to grab hold of it, but just as she went to throw it away something of interest caught her eye. It appeared to be a flyer for Tommy Doyle's party on Saturday night. Instead of disposing of it she passed it to Vincent.

"Are you going to this?" she said. "Leanne and Oliver are."

"I suppose so."

"You don't sound too enthusiastic."

"I'm not really." Vincent frowned. "I've heard a few things."

"Like what?"

Vincent had been learning forward on the bench, but now sat back and looked out across the schoolyard. "I've heard there's going to be drugs there." He shook his head slowly. "I'm not into that sort of thing."

"Drugs?" Emma's curiosity had been tweaked. "What sort of drugs?"

"I don't know. I don't care either."

"Who's bringing them?"

"Charlotte Angel, apparently."

"Is she going to be selling them?"

Vincent's looked concerned. He was not happy about Emma's apparent fascination with the topic.

"Why do you want to know?" he asked.

Emma shrugged her shoulders. "I just wondered."

"You 'just wondered'?" Vincent furrowed his brow. "Why?"

Emma suddenly felt uncomfortable. She and Vincent were clearly not on the same wavelength. She tried to explain herself. "It's not that I want to buy any," she said in a sheepish voice. "I've just wondered sometimes what it would be like to try drugs." She raised her eyebrows. "Haven't you ever thought about it?"

"No." Vincent shook his head. "I can't think of anything worse. Why would you even consider it?"

This was a really hard question for Emma to answer. She had never told anyone about how her mind sometimes tormented her with its compulsions and erratic thought processes.

"I would like to be able to clear my mind at times. Sometimes there's a lot going on and I'd like to replace certain thoughts with other thoughts," she said in an attempt at an explanation.

"What's that meant to mean?"

"It means my cerebral cortex could do with replacing its current sensory impulses with more stimulating neural processes. That's all," she said causally, smiling at him.

"Oh, come on, Em! You know I'm not a scientist." Vincent grinned at his friend's attempt to tease him. "You know what I'm asking."

Emma chose her words carefully and gave an explanation, as best she could, without giving too much away. "I suppose I wonder what all the fuss is about." She shrugged her shoulders and lowered her head. "I'm not interested in *doing* any drugs. I've just thought about it."

"OK." Vincent realised that Emma clearly did not want to talk about it anymore. He thought it best to leave it at that. It was definitely not worth arguing about, that was for certain. He was about to start a new topic of conversation when a ball hit him squarely on the side of the head. The pain set in immediately and he was in no doubt that it had been propelled extremely hard. Whether or not it had been an accident, he didn't yet know. As he regained his senses Vincent looked around to see who had thrown the ball.

It was Josh Hanger, one of the hardest kids in school. His reputation had been well earned. Five fights, with no losses. With his large build and scowling face, he looked tough as well. He was certainly not one to be messed with. Well, until now.

"What the hell...?" Vincent stood up angrily. "You did that on purpose."

Josh sniffed. "I might or I might not have done," he said. He turned up the palms of his hands. "Who knows?"

Vincent was not about to accept this as an answer. It was clearly a provocation, for which he would react to. "Don't screw with me!" He took a long stride towards the antagonist. "I'm not taking that from you!"

"Why, what are you going to do about it?" Two lengthy steps were quickly taken so that the two were face to face. "Think you're tough, do you?"

The battle lines had been drawn. Both of them fixed their gaze steadily on the other boy. Neither of them was about to back down. This could only go one way.

What Vincent was going through at home was bad enough, but being bullied elsewhere was not going to be tolerated. Although he would always back down when confronted by his stepfather, it still made him angry. While he was at home he had to accept the acts of aggression towards him, but that was not the case at school. If ever there was a time to make a stand it was now.

Vincent was not normally the type to get into fights. When he was younger he had got into a few minor scraps, but other than that he had never found himself in a situation resulting in violence. He did not bother others, so no one pestered him. The fact that he was big built undoubtedly helped to keep potential antagonists at bay.

Josh Hanger only loved one thing more than fighting, and that was the reputation he had earned for doing it. The other pupils knew that he was willing and able to hurt them whenever the opportunity arose. If he was in a bad mood he would take it out on someone else and they would rarely fight back. When someone had something that he wanted, like a chocolate bar, it was his for the taking. Fear could be a useful tool.

This situation, however, was not going how Josh expected. The person with whom he had hit the ball was of a large build, but that did not usually bother Josh. All he had to do normally was show he was prepared to use violence to meet his ends. His victim would always back down, until now.

The anger started to boil up inside of Vincent. He had endured years of being subjected to a jab to the ribs, a kick to the leg and a slap round the head. There was no way he was about to allow such physical ill-treatment at school. Quite simply, he did not have to take it.

As Vincent stood there, sizing up his opponent, he worked out how he could win the fight. All it would take was a sharp left jab to the nose, followed by a right hook to the eye to see him take the advantage. Half a dozen more punches, delivered to the head, should finish off his target. There would be no holding back and no risk of defeat.

Josh's plan was to spit in the face of his adversary, followed by a head butt to the bridge of the nose. This would be followed by grabbing hold of the collar to lower the target into a defenceless position and then bring the knee up to the jaw repeatedly. Mercy was not an option.

They both took aim. Like two coiled snakes, they prepared to strike. It was just a matter of who would launch their attack first.

"Don't even think about it!" The teacher spoke in an authoritative voice. "If either of you so much as raises a finger to the other one you'll be expelled immediately."

Mr Wall was a large man whose persona matched his physical stature. He had an overbearing presence his voice was forceful and booming. His features reflected his no-nonsense approach to authority, with his scowling brow and tight lips. He looked more like a sergeant major in the army than a schoolteacher. In fact, when it came to administering discipline his actions were almost as military as his appearance.

Mr Wall stood in between the two belligerent pupils, forming a human barrier to separate the warring parties. Neither of the boys would dare attempt to break through the formidable partition before them. Any attempt to do so would undoubtedly result in a severe punishment.

Vincent and Josh scowled at one another round the side of the intervening teacher. They both realised that the altercation was over and the option of it escalating to a fight was out of the question. It was simply a matter of who would walk away first, but Mr Wall made that decision for them. He had a pretty good idea which one of them had started the commotion.

"Hanger, get out of here now!" A rigid finger pointed in the direction he should go. "And make it quick!"

At that Josh reluctantly made his exit, but not before firing one final threat at his opponent. "I'll see you later."

"I know." Vincent spoke through clenched teeth. "I'll be looking for you."

At that, the incident came to an end. Josh disappeared into the distance, closely watched by Mr Wall to ensure he did not return. The teacher then left, leaving an uneasy peace in his wake.

Emma walked up behind Vincent who continued to stare after Josh. "That was intense." She put a calming hand on her friend's shoulder. "You OK?"

"Yeah." Vincent continued to glare in front of him. "I'm fine."

Emma took a moment to study him and then removed her hand. She knew he was not 'fine' at all, but thought it better not to drag out the situation by further discussion. In all the years she had known Vincent, she had never seen him behave like that, but she was not about to question his actions. Things were better left as they were.

Chapter 3

There was a stillness in the living room interrupted only by a dull, blue hue emanating through the window from the early evening twilight outside. A lone individual sat on the sofa, unmoving and indifferent to the low hum emitting from the television set. The atmosphere in the room had been one of cheerless gloom for the last hour or so, until the quiet was interrupted, but not for the better.

The hairs stood up on the back of Oliver's neck. A chill shivered its way through his veins. A feeling of unease troubled his mind. Once again, these afflictions were caused by the arrival of his father.

Oliver had felt his abuser walk into the room. He could sense Brian's heartless, cold stare on him. It made him feel sick and he swallowed painfully. He did not need to look at his tormentor to know what evil thoughts were being processed in the sick individual's mind. The man's illness was deep-rooted and always prevalent in his thinking.

In an act of self-preservation, Oliver immediately stood up to escape, but Brian intervened. "Where are you going?"

"Out."

"Out where?"

"The park."

Brian eyed Oliver suspiciously. For a moment, he felt as though his son's sudden departure was due to his presence, as though his arrival had instilled a feeling of anguish in the son he loved. He was sure this could not be the case.

Although Brian was a cruel and sick individual, his opinion of himself was one of high regard. He considered himself to be a loving father who was extremely protective of his son. Of course, he knew that paedophilia and incest were illegal, but in his warped mind they should not be outlawed. To him it was just his way of showing affection.

Brian attempted to persuade his son to stick around. "Why don't you stay here? We could have some father, son time." He smiled warmly, but his eyes were cold. "Just you and me. Like when we used to watch the football together."

"No thanks." The reply was subdued and awkward.

"Why?"

"I've arranged to meet my friends at the park. I can't let them down."

Brian tried to think of something more to say. He thought his son would want to spend time with him and the perplexed expression on his face reflected his bewilderment. He felt slightly hurt at being deserted; it almost made him feel as though he was the problem.

Oliver realised that his lie might just have worked. His father seemed to have conceded quite easily, so he started to shuffle his way out of the room. As he made his way past Brian he grimaced in expectation of the bodily contact that normally came his way, but this time it did not occur. For some reason he was allowed to get away without being molested.

As Oliver grabbed his coat he looked over his shoulder to see if his father had followed him, but the hall was empty. Realising he had escaped unscathed he quickly made his way out of the front door, closing it sharply behind him. It was a dull evening, but Oliver was glad to have left the house. He had not arranged to meet any of his friends at the park, but decided to go there anyway, to get away for a while.

As he headed towards his place of sanctuary he started to process what had just happened. It was as if his father had sensed his distress and backed away. Normally nothing would hold back the sick man, but something had caused a temporary cessation of the abuse. This was unusual and unexpected. It certainly required further thought.

Brian had been left alone in the living room. He was dumfounded by his son's reaction, wanting to leave as soon as he had entered the room. Deep in the back of his mind he wondered if it was because of him. This would be utterly shocking if that was the case.

If questioned, Brian would fervently declare that he loved his son deeply. In his deranged mind, he believed he had never done anything damaging to the body and mind of his tormented offspring. Obviously, this was not the case, but he simply did not recognise anything wrong with the abuse he had inflicted on his child. His ignorance about the depravity of his own actions found him puzzling over why he had been deserted and wondering if he was in any way culpable. This self-appraisal would probably not last long, though, and he would undoubtedly relapse back to his old ways.

"You can tell your father that he can cook his own dinner tonight." Leanne's mother pulled her travel bag over her shoulder. "I asked him to sort out that mess in the garage and it's all still there. If he can't do something as simple as that for me then why should I cook for him? It's about time he did something helpful around here for a change. God knows I do enough already."

"Where are you going?" Leanne's response was subdued.

"I'm going to Aunt Janet's for the evening."

"Is there anything for me to eat?"

"Your father can sort that out too."

At that, Sarah swiftly turned and made her exit. There was no consideration of how hungry her daughter might be because that was the least of her concerns. Her only intention was to target her husband with spite, and she did not care how she delivered her package of malevolence to him. She was too blinded by her own anger to realise the harm she was doing to her child by using her as a messenger for her hate.

Leanne did not want to be embroiled in such a nasty episode. It was bad enough having to witness her parents behave the way they did to each other, but to be a part of it only made it worse. Having to pass on their sentiments of anger to each of them made her feel they thought it was coming from her. She did not want to convey such bitterness.

After taking a while to think about how she should deal with her dilemma, Leanne decided it would be best to lie to her father. Telling him her mother was too busy to do the cooking would be more preferable than telling him she had not cooked the dinner out of spite. Refusing to pass on any unpleasantness would be the more civilised option. In fact, she would even pass on her mother's non-existent apology, for good measure.

In most households who prepared dinner would normally be a flexible matter, but not in this fractured home. Who was responsible for cooking and when was written down on a calendar on the wall, so that oversights could not occur. This was not just to avoid any misunderstanding, but to confirm who was in the right if someone did not fulfil their responsibilities.

To make things even easier, Leanne made a start on the washing up. She knew her father would be home any minute, which was why she did not begin cooking herself. Shortly afterwards, she heard the front door open. The animosity soon started again.

"Where is she?" Paul walked into the kitchen and looked around. "Am I missing something here?"

"Mum's gone to Aunt Janet's." Leanne went out of her way to sound cheerful. "She apologised but said she didn't have the time to cook."

"But it's Friday. She cooks the dinner on a Friday." Paul pointed a finger towards the calendar. "What's the point in having it written down if she's going to ignore it?"

"I'm sure she'll make up for it and cook on one of your nights."

"That's not good enough. She's supposed to cook this evening."

Paul slammed his leather briefcase down on the kitchen table, sending its contents sprawling across the surface. He grabbed his mobile hurriedly searched through the contacts. He held the handset to his ear and paced around the kitchen. It was no surprise to Leanne that his attempt to communicate with her mother had resulted in failure.

"She's turned her phone off. I knew it." He took a moment to think about how he was going to deal with the situation and then turned his attention to his daughter. "I'm not accepting this. I'm going to the bar to get something to eat. You can tell your mother when she gets in that she owes me the money for dinner. I don't see why I should pay for a meal that she's meant to be cooking."

This was not what Leanne wanted, but at the same time she had fully expected it. Her optimistic attempts to try and quell the situation had been futile. Even though she had not finished the washing up she dried her hands and turned away from the sink to face her father.

"Are you going to be out all night, Dad?" she asked sadly.

"I don't know." Paul was fastening the buttons on his coat, ready to leave. "Do you know when she'll be back?"

"She said she'd be there for the night."

"Well, in that case I'll stay out all night too."

At that Paul darted out of the kitchen. Within seconds the front door could be heard slamming shut. A familiar silence filled the house; like after all the other storms that had passed through before.

Leanne stood for a long moment feeling downbeat and vulnerable. There had been no avoiding what had just come to pass, but that was the norm these days. Not only did she regularly witness such conflict, but she was increasingly dragged into it. Her participation made things worse, especially when she tried to use her involvement in an attempt to resolve her parents' issues. Such acts of desperation were invariably ineffective.

Even though the source of the conflict had both left the house, Leanne decided she did not want to be there either. This desolate and loveless home was sometimes such a bitter place it felt more like a morgue than a sanctuary. She grabbed her coat from the back of a chair and picked up a packet of biscuits as a derisory replacement for dinner. With a quick glance at the unfinished washing up and the scattered contents of her father's briefcase, she left the house. Anywhere was better than here.

As Vincent entered the hall, he became aware of a rather irate conversation between his mother and stepfather who were in the living room. He decided it was best to stay clear, so he began to make his way up the stairs. He did not intend to get involved in something that might be detrimental to him. Unfortunately, his footsteps had been detected.

"Vincent!" His mother called out. "Come in here!"

Jack added, "Hurry up!"

Vincent stopped where he was and his shoulders slumped. He turned around and retraced his steps back down the stairs. When he reached the living room he hovered reluctantly in the doorway.

Fiona was sitting on the settee with an angry expression on her face, while Jack was lounging in an armchair, staring at him menacingly. The only person in the room who did not seem annoyed with him was his baby sister, Jade, who was soundly asleep in a carry cot next to the coffee table. Every indication pointed to him being in trouble and he rolled his eyes exaggeratedly. This did not go down well.

"Don't stand there with that attitude!" Fiona held up a piece of paper with the words 'maths exam' written at the top. "Do you want to explain this?"

This was met with a shrug of the shoulders and a raise of the eyebrows. Vincent knew that this chastisement was coming, but could not do much about it. He had never been a grade-A student and only occasionally managed a B. However, scoring an F in an exam was extremely rare for him and his mark in this test was not about to go unchallenged.

Fiona's questions reeled off in succession. "Didn't you do your homework? Did you not understand the questions in the exam? Why have you stopped trying at school?" She slammed the test sheet into the coffee table. "This isn't good enough."

Vincent could not bring himself to answer her questions because he did not like the answers. He had not done his homework and he did not understand the questions. Worst of all, he had stopped trying at school. There was simply no defence of his actions. At least that is what he thought. In fact, there were a number of truthful answers that he could have given that would have exonerated him.

The reason Vincent had not done his homework was because, for the months leading up to the exam, his mother and stepfather had been arguing even more than usual about the financial situation in the household. He was just not able to concentrate while there was a ruckus was going on downstairs. Ornaments thrown, insults hurled and the occasional back of the hand to the side of the face had led to him neglecting the school assignments he had brought home, including maths. As a result, he found that he had understood very few of the questions in the exam. But this was not his only burden.

Human beings always think more about the things that are most significant to them. People are not concerned about the itch in their foot when they have chronic toothache. English, history, geography and maths will never be as significant to a person as pain, anguish and suffering when the body and mind are going through turmoil. No one cares about Pythagoras's theory when they have a bruised eye, just as they have little interest in the capital city of Peru when they have heard their mother crying throughout the previous night.

The worse Vincent's home life had become the more his schoolwork suffered. As much as he knew what was affecting him, he could not bring himself to say anything about it to his mother. And certainly not his stepfather. He was quite sure that they would think he was trying to pass the blame for his own shortcomings on to them. Also, it would be extremely difficult to get sympathy from them both if they were not aware they were the cause of the problem.

Vincent had no choice but to take the admonishment from the people who were largely to blame for the situation. It was like being punched in the face and having to hear the aggressor complain about sore knuckles. Nothing about it was fair, but that was something he was getting used to.

After reprimanding him for some time, Fiona turned her attention to cleaning the windows. Jack made his way into the kitchen to fetch a beer, but not before giving his stepson a whack around the back of the head. The shouting and finger pointing were replaced by calm. Life carried on as if nothing had happened. Things were not at all as they should be though.

Vincent could not help but feel sorry for himself. He knew that he had been hard done by and felt powerless to do anything about it. Sadness and suffering, however, can quickly turn into anger and resentment, but that would only make things worse. There was no point in staying there with such feelings of rage. It was not as if he could take his temper out on his stepfather or vent his fury at his mother. With no way to unburden his emotions, leaving the scene of his despair seemed the only available course of action.

Vincent grabbed his coat, made his way out of the front door and was gone. He would, of course, be back, and things would undoubtedly be no different on his return, but even a short respite would be a welcome break from the wretchedness that he was going through. In the meantime, though, he would just have to let the heat burning within cool down in its own time.

Karen was diligently making sure that all her chores were done as quickly as possible. It was coming to the end of her day and she was completing her final tasks. These were not household errands though, but her responsibilities at the call centre. She needed to catalogue all of the phone calls she had received, register the complaints that had been made and make a list of the customers who had been successfully dealt with. After that she had to send all of the data to the relevant departments so that it could be processed. She could then log out of the computer and that would be one more shift finished. Another laborious stint done and another day's pay earned. Well, sort of.

Karen had a little less than thirty minutes to get to the bar where she worked in the evenings. Once there she would have to get changed, put the dirty glasses into the dishwasher, clean the messy tables, wipe down the bar and then serve customers for another six hours. If she was lucky she would get time to have something to eat while on the go for the entire shift.

This was just another day in the life of this struggling mother. It was an act of self-sacrifice and selflessness, and never did she expect any acknowledgement for her unwavering endeavour. This was the existence of a true champion of society; the legendary single working mum. Sadly, sometimes giving everything is not enough.

Unbeknown to Karen, regardless of her effort and resolve, she was needed considerably more elsewhere. As good as a mother that she was, she could not be in two places at the same time.

Emma was lying in the middle of the park gazing up at the sky. She was there alone, but that was fine. Moments of solitude were not rare for her and she was used to being lonely. It was actually relaxing hearing only the softness of the wind and the sounds of nature.

As Emma slowly breathed in and out she raised her hands up above her, squinting as the sun shone through her fingers. For once she felt no need to make the space in between them the same size or make identical shapes. There was no compulsive urge to fulfil an unneeded obsession. Her mind seemed to be giving her a well-needed rest from her usual mental afflictions.

Feeling at peace within herself, Emma lowered her hands but continued looking up at the sky. After a while her attention was drawn to a group of eight small clouds that were clustered together way above her. There were eight. No more and no less. There were exactly eight.

It was at this point that something clicked in Emma's mind. She was not sure what it was, but it seemed to alter the route her once restful train of thought was travelling. It was an uncomfortable feeling, but she did not know what caused it or why. There was no feeling of danger or sickness and she felt no sadness or anger. Something was wrong, but she had no idea what.

In her uneasiness, Emma turned her gaze from the eight clouds and looked down at her hands that were now resting on her stomach. Then it happened. Horror gripped her. On the back of Emma's hands were scores of spiders crawling about all over them. They were only small, but there were enough of them to make her freeze with fear. It was as if she had lost her sense of touch, as she could not feel them even though they scurried across the hairs on her skin. All she was able to do was watch in terror as the eight-legged insects crept across her knuckles and in between her fingers.

After enduring the invasion upon her flesh for much too long, Emma managed to break free of her frozen state and take action. She started to scratch the backs of her hands erratically to get rid of the spiders. As she did so the skin begun to peel away and hot pain shot up through her arms. Although the stinging was excruciating, it was nothing compared to the torment in her mind. The feeling of having her body violated by the insects made her stomach churn. In a moment of despair, she screamed aloud and closed her eyes to shut out the agony. Then, finally, there was calm.

Time passed. Not a lot, but enough. When Emma finally took control of herself she slowly opened her eyes and looked at her hands. Much to her relief, all of the spiders were gone. Not a trace of them remained apart from the scratches that she had inflicted on herself. The relief of being rid of the unwelcome invaders was so overwhelming that it shut out the physical pain that she had inflicted on herself. Her reprieve had not come a moment too soon.

It was not surprising that the infestation of spiders had dispersed, because they had never been there in the first place. Emma's mental health problems were not limited to obsessively having to make shapes and count numbers. On other occasions she also suffered from hallucinations and this was, naturally, very distressing for her. To make things worse, it was normally spiders that she saw and the fact that she suffered from arachnophobia made this unbearable.

Emma's visions were no different to those the brain creates when a person is falling asleep. When someone is drifting off into unconsciousness their mind produces random images of objects, people and places. Of course, they are actually in bed and what they see is not there. Their spontaneous thought processes create mental pictures in their sleep, just like hallucinations create a non-existent image while awake.

It is not surprising that the human brain does such a thing. Every night it generates visions, so it is to be expected that, in some people, it does the same during the day. This does not mean the person suffering from the illusory images is insane. They are just different.

Emma had been experiencing hallucinations for a few years now. She knew she had some kind of problem, but had never been able to work out what it was as she was not able to talk to anyone about it. When she had first started seeing images she was convinced they were real, but after a number of occasions when they seemingly disappeared as quickly as they had materialised she begun to realise they didn't exist.

Sometimes, the spiders that Emma saw were small, whereas on other occasions they were much larger. The bigger ones were actually more favourable in a strange kind of way. Quite simply, there were no insects that big where she lived, so she realised they were not genuine. It was when she saw a multitude of miniscule arachnids that she really felt nauseous. After all, there was always a chance that these ones could be real.

Unfortunately for Emma, the sight of the spiders on her hands had caused her a great deal of distress. Although the episode was over, the anxiety still gripped hold of her and she could not help shaking uncontrollably. Her hands trembled and her jaw chattered until it ached at the joints. There seemed to be no let up and no apparent means of aid coming her way any time soon.

All Emma really needed was for someone to be there for her. Anyone would do. If she had someone to talk to about her problems, the burden she was carrying would be eased. Just one person to tell her that everything was alright and that she was not alone. That was all.

If Karen had been there she would have put her arm around her daughter and asked her what was wrong. She would have provided the comfort Emma needed, offered her support and the promise of a brighter future. Plans would have been made and provisions put in place. Everything would be fine.

Karen was not there, though. No one was. So nothing was going to get better. Emma would have to carry on suffering alone.

Vincent and Oliver were walking along the path towards the park in no great urgency to reach their destination. They had come across each other while leaving Sanctuary Green and, after a brief discussion, headed in the direction of their usual meeting point. As they idly strolled along they chatted unenthusiastically about the weekend's football results, rather than divulge what was really going on in their minds.

It was no surprise that neither of them wanted to talk about the abuse they were enduring at home. Not only was it private to them, but it would also be embarrassing. It is extremely hard for young males to express their feelings if it shows them to be weak in some way. In a modern society this should not be the case, of course, but these two had never been taught how to put aside their insecurities and reveal to those around them how they felt. This is as sad as it is commonplace.

Oliver was not at fault because he didn't want to talk about the abuse he was suffering at the hands of his paedophile father. Starting a discussion, with any of his friends, about the sickening acts he had endured over the years was completely out of the question. He did not even know how he would start to explain how his only sexual encounters had been with a member of his family. Telling all was not an option, but talking about the fact that he was hurting certainly was, if he could only bring himself to do it.

Oliver would have loved to tell his friends that he was unhappy, but was too ashamed to. He was scared that they would ask questions that he would not want to answer. The abuse that he suffered at home was very private to him and he was not willing to talk about it to anyone. However, the stress he was suffering was certainly something he would have liked to get out in open to make himself feel better.

Having someone to listen to him would have been such a relief for Oliver. Telling someone that he could not sleep at night, without being pressed to give an explanation, would have helped to relieve some of his anguish. Simply talking about how he wished his life was different without having to give details would help. Unfortunately, he had to suffer in silence, just like his friend.

Vincent normally liked talking about football, but on this occasion he would rather have been trying to disperse the rage within him. He had suffered violence at the hands of his stepfather for so long now that he was almost always on edge. It was like he was constantly simmering and about to come to the boil. The smallest of things would make him lose his temper and vent his fury. Circumstances over which he had no control would invariably be met with a temperamental outburst. Someone accidently knocking into him in the school corridor or waiting for too long in a queue would regularly bring about a display of anger. He resented any incident that took away his control and he dealt with it in the only way he knew how.

Vincent's reliance on anger to solve situations was a result of the way he had witnessed his stepfather use it to control him. Jack would not only hit his stepson, but also heatedly raise his voice at him to get his way. A growling command to get the biscuits from the kitchen or a snarling demand to get out of his way would see his wishes granted. These lessons on how to influence others had been duly observed and the mindset acquired. The ability to expel his demons by setting them loose on others had been learnt by Vincent.

Unfortunately, the anger he was feeling inside him, at this moment, due to the reprimand he had received for failing his maths exam could not be directed at anyone else. There was no one in his way, nobody talking too loud or asking for trouble. He simply had to keep his wrath locked up within himself like a lion imprisoned in a cage. This was not a comfortable feeling.

So the two friends continued talking about football even though they would both have rather been talking about how they felt and unloading the burdens they were carrying. Each of them suppressed their feelings and attempted to hide their emotions. As much as they tried, they still could not help but show a glimmer of what was going on in their minds.

"He's not a good player and never will be. I hate him," said Oliver with disdain.

"I wouldn't even have him in the team. Waste of space," Vincent sneered.

Leanne approached the gates to the park. She had not deliberately chosen any particular destination, but had inadvertently found herself there. The entrance overlooked the whole of the grounds and, as she made her way through, she noticed Emma sitting on the grass in the distance. With a feeling of relief, she quickened her pace and headed towards her friend.

This moment of companionship would be very welcome. The two of them would be able to find solace in discussing their problems and sharing their feelings. Both of them were carrying a huge weight and having the chance to unload some of that burden would be a great relief. Neither of them would want to waste this opportunity to relieve their stress.

Leanne approached her friend with feigned happiness. "Hey, Em!"

"Hi." Emma forced a smile too and pulled her sleeves over her hands to hide the scratches.

Leanne sat down on the grass next to her friend. "How's things?"

"Been better, to be honest."

"Why, what's up?"

Emma took a deep breath and paused for a moment to think about her response. "I've been getting these weird headaches recently. My brain's been all over the place." She put her fingers to her temples in an exasperated manner. "It's like I'm not in control of what's going on in my head."

At that, she was interrupted. "I know what you mean. I hate it when I get headaches. Mind you, most of mine are caused by my parents."

"Yeah, but these aren't like that. I can't think straight and I don't know how to stop my mind from doing what it likes." Emma made a gesture with her hands as though her head was being crushed. "It's as though the world is closing in on me."

Leanne waited for her friend to finish talking and then continued talking about her own troubles. "My world is a disaster as well right now. My mum and dad don't even know I'm here." She put her hand up in front of her face in a gesture to check that she was actually there. "It's like I don't exist. I think if I disappeared off the face of the earth neither of them would notice."

At that, the two close friends continued pouring out their own problems without either of them listening to a word of what the other was saying. Neither of them acknowledged how bad the other felt and both of them failed to grasp the gravity of the other's predicament. When they needed an ear, all they got was a mouth.

Emma and Leanne both really wanted to unload their problems, but all they found themselves doing was taking on each other's burden. Instead of reducing the weight on their shoulders, they only increased their load. Neither of them was aware of what they were doing or how damaging it was. They were young and inexperienced, and in their naivety they were making things worse for each other. If only they understood that humans have two ears and one mouth, so they should listen twice as much as they talk.

Vincent and Oliver discovered Leanne and Emma in their usual spot in the park and immediately went over to join them. The quartet assumed their usual on their backs, with their bodies forming a cross. There was no outpouring of anguish and no one listened to the problems of another to alleviate their hardship. The conversation was menial and wasted.

"I don't think I'll watch the game tonight."

"I can't even be bothered to watch TV."

"I might go back home to bed."

"I don't know what I'm going to do."

"We are the most efficient species on the planet at communicating, but sometimes we are the most mute and deaf, and it's purely through choice." Mrs Reason sat on her desk at the front of the class with her legs crossed and her arms folded. "There are times when talking about our innermost feelings to those closest to us, or even a stranger, can help us no end, but it requires a person who is willing to talk and an individual who is ready to listen. These are two very simple things, but we regularly fail at them."

Mrs Reason slid off the desk and on to the floor. As she stood in amongst the pupils, she could not be seen by everyone in the classroom, of which she was fully aware of, however, she also knew that her voice would carry. She was used to not being seen, so she was adept at making herself heard.

"It is extremely hard for people to open up about their problems. Sometimes, it can make them feel vulnerable to let someone know that they are hurting or that they can't cope with what is going on in their life. They might have money difficulties, a complication with their private life or even a personal health problem, but they are too embarrassed, ashamed or shy to talk about it. So who can you turn to? Lots of people, hopefully, and they come into three categories: friends, family and trained professionals." Mrs Reason walked over to the white board at the front of the classroom and wrote the word 'YOU' on it. "So let's begin with the most important person, you. If you are a good friend you should be willing to be there for your friends and vice versa, because good friends don't judge and they don't mock, but they do listen. A good friend who is prepared to listen gives their time, attention and understanding. You should take a moment to think about whether you are that person. Are you?"

Mrs Reason looked at each of her pupil's faces as they inwardly pondered their own worth as friends. Some appeared confident, whereas others had a blank look on their faces. It was to be expected that not all of them were pleased with their self-appraisal. When she felt they had been given enough time to evaluate themselves she gave them a warning.

"There is one important thing you should all be mindful of. If you do find yourself talking to someone about your problems, or you're listening to them talk about their troubles, you must be aware that you are not a psychologist and most likely neither is the other person. Sometimes the advice that you could give, or be given, could do more damage than good. If someone is advised to break up with a partner or quit their job it could have dire consequences. That is why, sometimes, all you need to do is listen or be listened to. Remember, if someone is talking about their problems the discussion is about them, not you. A response is not always necessary."

There was a brief pause while she let her words sink in, before continuing with the lesson. "Your family are also a good option when it comes to discussing your problems. They, of course, might be the root of the problem or might not be around to talk to. Your parents might argue in front of you or one of them might have left home, but hopefully there might be someone around for you to confide in. If you have brothers or sisters they are probably living a similar life to you so they should be able to relate to what you are going through." She pointed to the word 'YOU' on the white board. "You should be willing to listen to them as well."

Again, Mrs Reason paused momentarily before continuing. "Also, you can talk to trained professionals. This could be counsellors, healthcare workers or even schoolteachers. We aren't here just to teach, but to guide as well. As for those who have had specific training in psychology, they can give invaluable advice." She tapped a laptop on her desk. "You can find phone numbers and addresses online or you can talk to anyone here in confidence. The help you need is not a million miles away."

Mrs Reason wrote two more words on the white board. 'Turning points' was underlined twice to stress the importance. She faced the class again and continued the lesson.

"All through your life you will reach junctions where you will need to make a decision that could either have a positive or negative effect on you. It could lead to something really outstanding, like starting a successful new business or beginning a fitness regime that will give you a healthy lifestyle. However, you might also make the wrong decision which could change your life for the worse. You might start smoking which could lead to premature death or you might choose to break the law and end up in prison." She pointed to the two words on the white board. "The next chapter of the book is all about 'turning points'."

Chapter 4

The music from the party carried across the streets. The sound of excited teens, laughing and joking, could also be heard as they descended from all directions on the large red house where the party was being held. There was only one place to be tonight.

Tommy Doyle certainly knew how to throw a party and being the son of rich parents meant that he had spared no expense. The trees in the large front garden were adorned with flashing lights and the house itself was decorated with colourful banners. The booming sound system had been hired for the evening and a DJ from a local club had been drafted in to control the music. There would also be a fireworks display later on in the night. The party promised to live up to the hype and all of those who were now arriving were expecting to have a fantastic time.

As the youngsters were making their way to the party, Vincent was sitting on a wall at the corner of the street watching them all closely. He was in no hurry to get there and was waiting for his friends to get to their arranged meeting point so that they could all arrive together. They were a tight-knit group and, although they were not individually shy, when it came to big events being together was essential. However, as Vincent scanned those arriving it was not only his friends he was looking out for.

The main target of Vincent's searching gaze was Josh Hanger. He knew his adversary would be going to the party and he wanted to make sure that he was ready for him. The last thing he wanted was to be taken by surprise and attacked out of the blue, so he kept his eye out to make sure that he would not be at a disadvantage.

"Vincent!"

The voice came from afar, but was familiar. Leanne had called out from end of the path as she and Oliver turned the corner. She waved her hand enthusiastically and raised a carrier bag in her other. It obviously contained alcohol in it and she wanted to show it off. It was no surprise that the youngsters would be drinking at the party, even though it was illegal.

"Hi guys." Vincent got down from the wall. "Where's Emma?"

"She's on her way. She said she had to get some money and buy stuff for the party." Oliver shrugged his shoulders to show he was ignorant of the fine details. "I'm not sure what she's getting though."

Leanne gave Vincent an exaggerated hug and kissed him briefly, but fully on the lips. It came out of nowhere and took him by surprise. He forced a smile to appease her, but could not hide his uneasiness. Although they were all physically affectionate towards each other, it never usually went beyond an arm around the shoulder or a kiss on the cheek.

As Leanne turned away to look out for Emma, Vincent glanced at Oliver who responded with a whisper. "She did the same to me." This was followed by a raise of the eyebrows.

Both lads stared at Leanne, who now had her back to them. She was wearing high heeled, red shoes and a short, tight fitting, black dress. She turned around to face them with an excited look on her face, but all they noticed was her revealing cleavage; her breasts were more on show than covered. Even her make-up was heavier than usual.

"I wish Em would hurry up." Leanne raised the bag with alcohol in. "I want to get started."

Oliver and Vincent smiled at her awkwardly and glanced sideways at one another. It was obvious that their friend was out to have fun tonight, and hoped there wouldn't be any repercussions. Although they cared about her deeply, they would not stand in her way if she wanted to do something she might later regret. She was, after all, her own person.

A strong, pungent smell wafted past the group of friends. None of them turned to see where it was coming from until a familiar voice called to them from behind. It was at that point the source became apparent.

"Hey guys." Emma stood there with a nonchalant expression. "How's it going?"

None of them answered. They stared at her with confounded looks on their faces. It was not what she was wearing that had grabbed their attention, but what she was doing.

"What?" Emma appeared displeased about the way she was being gawped at. "Have you never seen a cigarette before?"

The four friends had always accepted that they were all different and had their own personalities. Different views, tastes in music and fashion were never a problem, but none of them had ever smoked. It was just not what they did.

"What's all that about, Em?" Vincent pointed to the cigarette hanging from her mouth.

"I fancied a smoke." Emma shrugged her shoulders in an indifferent manner and pointed towards the red house. "It's a party, isn't it?"

"Yeah, I suppose we're here to have a good time." Leanne tried to justify her friend's actions. "We all have our own way of enjoying ourselves."

No one else spoke, until Oliver made an effort to get things moving. "Shall we get in there and start the night rolling?" He tried his best to look enthusiastic. "No point in standing here all night."

"Exactly."

"Yeah."

"Let's do this."

At which point the four of them made their way towards the booming sounds of the party, excited for what the night had in store for them. Some of them were more excited than others, but their intentions for the evening were vastly different. Decisions would be made in the coming hours that might affect them for the rest of their lives.

As the group made their way up the driveway to the large red house, Oliver glanced around at the girls arriving at the party. Some of them wore very short skirts and low-cut tops, revealing long legs and generous curves. He uncomfortably pushed his hands into his pockets at the sight and lowered his gaze. This was going to be a long night.

The four friends pushed their way through the large entrance of the house and towards the main living room which seemed to be the hub of the party, stopping occasionally to greet people they knew. They eventually found a space amongst the crowd, poured themselves a drink and began to enjoy the evening; for a while at least.

The party was well underway. Enthusiastic young people danced like no one was watching them and those who weren't dancing couldn't help moving to the beat. Although the music was really loud, laughter and screams could be heard above it. The atmosphere was wild, wonderful and wicked.

It was two hours into the party and Leanne had consumed rather a lot of alcohol, especially for her size and young age. She was starting to feel more than a bit tipsy and had even started to sway unsteadily, which had been noticed by her friends. Several times she had smiled at passing boys, some of whom she knew and others she did not. This normally shy girl was certainly not her usual self tonight.

With her revealing clothes and eagerness to draw attention to herself, Leanne was certainly getting noticed, and she liked it. Flicks of the hair and winks of the eye were certainly an effective method of gaining interest. Most of the boys responded with mirrored smiles and cheeky comments. Even some of the pupils from her school who had never said a word to her before conversed with her in a keen manner even if some of them did seem to spend rather too much time staring at her cleavage instead of her face. Leanne did not seem to think this was anything to be too concerned about; she was having too much fun to care.

With her confidence elevated to a higher level than usual, Leanne decided to take a walk around the large house to see who else she could find. She informed her friends that she was going for a wander and spiritedly made her way off. As she departed the three remaining friends looked at each other in concern.

There was a large gathering of people in the kitchen so Leanne decided that would be a good place to socialise. Most of the partygoers here were drinking alcohol and were more boisterous than the others in the rest of the house. Some couples were openly kissing, whereas others spoke to each other while making close bodily contact. This certainly appeared to be the place where she wanted to be, and that was confirmed when she heard a familiar voice.

"I'm glad you came."

Leanne turned her head to see who had spoken to her, but she was not given the chance to respond.

"I was starting to wonder if I was going to be bored to death by the usual people all night. It's about time someone interesting turned up."

Brad Jacobs made his introduction with a well-practised smile and rehearsed compliment. He gave his intended victim a quick kiss on the cheek and slid his hand down her back in a caressing gesture, just shy of being 'too much'. Every tried and tested move went as planned. When it came to implementing his well-drawn out schemes, Brad certainly knew what worked and he rarely got it wrong.

Leanne was taken in by Brad's words and actions. His smile made her heart melt and his verbal assault shattered any walls that she might have had defending her. All eye contact was designed to show that he was utterly fascinated by her. If there was an opportunity to give her a compliment he did so without hesitation. The whole contrived act was clockwork in motion.

Leanne felt great and it was all Brad's doing. He made her feel interesting, beautiful and, most of all, significant. That was a sensation that she had not experienced in a long time. When Leanne's parents were arguing they never noticed how much it upset her. Even if she was upset they were too busy shouting at each other to be aware of it. She was regularly ignored, as were her feelings. It was so nice to actually be the centre of attention for once.

With her emotions all over the place, Leanne felt utterly drawn to Brad. He could do no wrong. There was no place she would rather be than with him right now. In fact, she would go anywhere with him and, in a matter of time, she probably would. It is so much easier when the prey comes to the hunter. No chase is necessary and the game is on.

"Do you want to see the main bedroom?"

That final line signified the end of the performance. Not a word was spoken in response; just a nod of the head. As Leanne was led away by the hand all that was left was the final act and the show would come to an end.

The flick of the light switch instantly resulted in the illumination of the bedroom. Leanne lay under the duvet, naked and unmoving. As she glanced over her shoulder she noticed that Brad was already putting on his trousers. No words were exchanged.

It seemed the pleasantries had now ceased. No more compliments were awarded and there were zero attempts at physical interaction. Feelings were ignored and sentiments no longer expressed. The atmosphere had become barren.

As Brad buttoned up his shirt he paid no attention to his conquest. He headed for the door without looking back or uttering a word. It was like he had been alone in the room and there was no one else to be concerned about. There was no consideration for Leanne's feelings whatsoever.

Leanne sat up, covering her naked breasts with the duvet. She had so much to say, but she was not given time to speak. The door had already closed. She was now alone, as usual.

At first Leanne thought that maybe Brad had gone to the toilet. He might even have gone to get them both a drink. She was sure he would be back soon. Her thoughts were hopeful more than expectant. After about twenty minutes she accepted the obvious. She too then got dressed and left the room.

"I would've knocked him out." The words were slurred, but spoken in anger. "He thinks he's hard, but he's nothing."

A number of partygoers were listening to Josh Hanger's version of events as he described his altercation with Vincent. Not all of the people within earshot were his friends; in fact, there were very few individuals whom he could consider to be that close to. He was not the most likeable person around. The majority of those who were focusing their attention on him were doing so simply because he was talking so loudly. If truth be known, they were not even that interested in what he was saying.

The few friends of Josh's who were there started making their own observations.

"He wouldn't have stood a chance against you."

"I know."

"He's big, but I reckon you could do him easily."

"He's not that big."

"So why didn't you whack him?" It was a fair question asked by an outsider to the group who had been listening in.

"Mr Wall stopped me." Josh's face twisted into a snarling expression. "I'm on my last warning at school; that's the only reason I didn't bang him out."

"He's here."

"What?"

A finger pointed through a large double doorway leading into the living room. The room was crowded with people, but the focal point of their gaze could be clearly observed in amongst them. Unaware that he was being watched, Vincent stood talking to a friend from his football team, oblivious to the fact that his evening was about to be interrupted.

Josh did not wait to act. He left his friends without saying a word. It took them a moment to realise he was going straight for his target, but then they eagerly followed. They knew what was coming, as they had seen it many times before, and it was not something they wanted to miss.

The partygoers in the living room were pushed aside as Josh forcibly made his way through them. His friends enthusiastically jostled behind so as to obtain a good view of the impending fight. The surrounding revellers soon realised that something was occurring and they too turned their attention to the centre of the disturbance.

"Do you want to sort this out?" Josh said heatedly. His body language was menacing and both of his fists were tightly clenched. Josh's heart was racing as he steadied himself to unleash a flurry of devastating blows. He positioned himself in a sideways stance ready to throw his first punch, poised to inflict the maximum amount of damage.

Vincent had seen this many times before. That look in the eye, those gritted teeth and the intent in the voice had been exposed to him regularly over the years. He knew from experience when someone was about to be violent towards him. He did not intend to be the victim this time though.

There had been many times when Jack had thrown punches, aimed kicks and hurled objects at Vincent, but he had always had to endure it. He knew that fighting back against a fully grown adult was simply not an option. Every blow to the face, ribs and stomach had always been suffered without retaliation. Fighting back would have only meant more punishment. This was how it had always been, until now. Josh Hanger was big, but no adult. He was hard, but not unbeatable. His reputation was formidable, but that would not matter one bit today.

The punch landed straight on the nose, immediately breaking it, sending blood down on to the lips. Due to his drunken state, Josh had not seen it coming. He certainly was not aware that it had happened either. As his unconscious body slammed against the floor all that could be heard around him were spontaneous gasps from astonished onlookers.

Vincent stood tall, looking down on his victim. All around him people stared in awe. Even Josh's friends stayed unmoving, not daring to get involved. No one approached the victor or the defeated.

Adrenaline coursed through Vincent's veins, but all he could feel right now was elation. For once he was not the sufferer, but instead the survivor. Not only had the encounter ended with him not experiencing pain for once, but in its place was a sensation of euphoria. He liked this feeling a lot.

Vincent looked around him proudly. Most of the youngsters had a look of shock on their faces. The more sadistic individuals grinned at the spectacle. Nevertheless, no one said anything to him.

After realising that he had achieved exactly what he had set out to do this evening, Vincent decided it was time to leave. He stepped over Josh's unconscious body and made his way out of the living room. Everything had gone to plan and there could not possibly be any impending consequences for his actions. At least that's what he thought.

A number of people had now left the party, but it was still going strong. Those with more stamina continued to dance, whereas some of the more intoxicated youngsters were sprawled around the house in various states of responsiveness. On the top floor there was a concentrated gathering of people in and around the bathroom which seemed to Emma a rather strange place to congregate.

She had been standing on a lower landing when she had noticed the small crowd of people huddled together and decided to see what was going on. As she made her way up the stairs she squeezed past a number of other partygoers. As she reached the top floor she unexpectedly received a lash to the face.

"Sorry!" The apology was given immediately and without reservation. "I didn't see you there."

Kim Warnock had been trying unsuccessfully to wrap her scarf around her neck, but in the process had lashed Emma around the face with it. Even now she was trying to twist and turn the garment so that it fit her perfectly. It all appeared to be rather clumsy and pointless.

Emma rubbed her stinging eye as she watched Kim struggling to fit the scarf around her neck in a manner that she found acceptable. She kept undoing it and then making another unsuccessful attempt to reapply it, even though there was little wrong with it in the first place.

"What are you doing?" Emma asked, "Is there something wrong with you?"

The answer to the latter question could hardly be answered as there actually was something wrong with Kim. She could not help but be rather clumsy and awkward with her actions. It was not her fault. No one can help the way they are born. In fact, she was known around the school for being somewhat strange.

Kim Warnock was a small girl, to the point of frailty. She seemed to have no presence about her and even her voice was so quiet it was almost a whisper. She was not the type of person who would stand out in a crowd, physically or audibly. It was her mannerisms that got her noticed.

Kim had a reputation for being rather eccentric. She would often be observed around the school doing peculiar things with her hands or completing strange rituals like balancing cans of drink on top of each other. Not only were her physical habits odd, but her speech skills were also somewhat strange. At times she would be quiet and introverted, but if someone was to strike up a conversation with her she could talk non-stop about quite insignificant subjects without giving the other person a chance to speak. In fact, it was surprising that she had turned up at the party as she was rarely seen out with friends.

Eventually, Kim let her scarf hang limply over her shoulders in probably the untidiest of her efforts yet.

"You're weird," said Emma, before walking off.

Kim took a moment to think about their brief encounter and shrugged her shoulders dismissively. She then carried on trying to adjust her scarf.

The group of people gathered around the bathroom at the top of the house seemed either a lot more relaxed than the rest of the partygoers or vastly more excited. Some of them were very chilled and laid back, whereas others appeared to be extremely chatty.

Emma entered the bathroom and glanced around at the occupants. Some sat on the floor, unmoving and seemingly staring straight out into space. Others were speaking really quickly and appeared overly cheerful. It was when she noticed what was on the corner of the sink that she realised why.

There, displayed for all to see, was an assortment of drugs. Pills, cocaine and cannabis were lined up like sweets for people to take their pick, for a price, of course. Bags were filled with coloured tablets, lines of powder were displayed in parallel doses, and joints rolled neatly waiting to be smoked. Whatever you wanted was yours, if you had the money and the inclination.

"What's your pleasure?" The words were spoken in a friendly manner. "I've got loads of white, but I'm running low on green."

Charlotte Angel was one of those people who everyone saw around town, but few knew who she was. She was regularly seen on street corners, in the park or hanging around the shops. Everyone knew of her, but very few people actually *knew* her.

Charlotte's inconspicuous manner was quite deliberate. She had been dealing drugs for a number of years, even though she had only just turned twenty years old. Her older brother had been involved in the illicit trade long before she had become a part of it and her eventual inclusion into the shady business had almost been inevitable. The attraction of large sums of money vastly outweighed the risk of a lengthy prison sentence.

Nothing about Charlotte stood out, and that was intentional. She did not wear expensive jewellery or flash clothes. Her usual unassuming attire was a T-shirt and jeans. Even her car was a relatively old family saloon, dotted with rust and dents. The fact that she had never been caught showed that her approach was working.

As she gave her sales pitch, Charlotte's true outgoing self came to the fore. "The coke is good. It hasn't got loads of crap mixed into it. The pills are awesome. I had a couple last week." Everything was said in an amicable manner and with a warm smile. "As for the weed, well, it's weed."

Emma looked at all the products that were for sale. She was not sure what all of them actually were, or, more importantly, what they would do to her. At no point in her life had she experimented with drugs. It was all very bewildering.

"First time is it?" said Charlotte.

"Yeah, it is."

"That's cool." Charlotte spoke in a reassuring voice. "Well, there's no point in going for anything too wild. You don't want to take something you're not ready for. It's probably best you go for a line of coke. You can have the first one for nothing, to see if you like it."

Emma smiled and nodded awkwardly. She felt slightly uncomfortable, but was sure this was what she wanted. Most of the time her mind was full of disturbing sensory incursions that were beyond her control and the chance to replace those with more favourable sensations would be a welcome change, even if she did not know exactly what to expect. It seemed risky, but she would give it a go.

Although there were already three lines of cocaine on the side of the sink, Charlotte got a small bag out of her pocket and poured some out on the edge of the bath. She got a bank card, dabbed it on the powder and shaped it into a long horizontal column. She then stood back and held out a small straw. What needed to be done now was obvious.

Emma moved forward hesitantly. Without even looking at Charlotte she took the straw and knelt down next to the bath. As she eyed the line of cocaine she braced herself and tried to empty her mind. Then she went for it.

It did not take long for the drug to take effect. Emma felt on top of the world and she made no attempt at hiding it. She joined in on people's conversations who she did not even know and she danced wildly by herself in the middle of the living room. Where once in her mind were unwanted thought processes there were now feelings of euphoria and ecstasy. There simply seemed to be no downside, for the time being anyway.

The party was coming to an end. There was vomit on the floor, drink spillages in every room and a general mess throughout the house. A few of the partygoers had passed out on the furniture, whereas some of those who had taken some form of drug use were still as hyper as they were at the beginning of the evening. Some would crash for the night, whereas others had begun to unsteadily make their way home.

Oliver found himself walking around the large house without any particular destination or intention of doing anything. He passed the occasional kissing couple, a girl who was sitting on the stairs crying and a guy who was wondering around in his underpants. Then something caught his eye that made him stop and give it his full attention.

Oliver was on the second floor of the house and noticed that one of the bedroom doors was ajar. As he moved closer he peeked through the gap. There, on a bed, seemingly fast asleep was a young girl. What he saw would certainly warrant a more thorough investigation.

After taking a moment to look up and down the hall, Oliver stepped into the room and pushed the door back so that it was only about an inch ajar. Enough light was now being let into the room for him to see, but not enough for anyone else to look in. He slowly made his way over to the bed to see who it was who was asleep on it. On getting closer, he recognised the girl.

Diane Deacon was in the same year as Oliver at school. They were in the same history and science classes, but they had never spoken before. They were probably both aware of each other's existence, but that was it.

Diane lay there with her legs were slightly apart. Her skirt had inadvertently ridden up to the top of her thighs and her underwear was partially visible, leaving her quite exposed. Due to her drinking too much alcohol she had passed out, unaware of the precarious situation she had left herself in.

Diane was an attractive girl. Many of the boys at the school had asked her on a date, a few she had agreed to, and others she had not. It appeared that she hadn't formed a relationship with any of them. One day a guy would get lucky and he would certainly be the envy of his peers.

Oliver looked towards the door and took a moment to listen if anyone was close. It seemed that no one was around, so he sat on the bed next to Diane. Very slowly, he moved his hand towards her legs. He closed his mind and turned off any compassion he might have felt for her. With his heart thumping, he stepped over a line that no person should ever cross.

In one of the worst acts any human being can commit, Oliver sexually assaulted Diane. Although the crime was of a sexual orientation it was, in fact, derived by the desire for power over an individual. He did it not so much for the carnal satisfaction, but because he wanted to have control over the person.

For many years, Oliver had suffered the same type of assault at the hands of his sick father. This had made him feel insecure and helpless. However, now that he found himself in a situation where he had power over someone, and his victim was at his mercy, he felt like he was the one in control. His mind had been corrupted over the years as he had never faced up to what he had been going through and sought the help he needed. Now someone else was paying for it.

The sound of footsteps alerted Oliver that someone was coming, and he stood up quickly. As he peered through the gap in the doorway he noticed someone walk past the room. With a final glance at his victim, he realised it was time to leave.

As Oliver closed the door behind him he looked around to check no one had seen him. Satisfied there was no chance of him being identified he made his way off. There was no consideration for what he had done or for the feelings of his victim. All that he knew right now was a feeling of power that he had callously stolen from someone who did not deserve such disgusting treatment. His desires were satisfied, but at a cost.

A group of girls and boys were standing outside the school gym. They were joking and laughing about the party, exchanging pictures and videos. It did not take long for them to start gossiping about certain individuals.

"Oh my God, did you hear about Brad Jacobs and that Leanne girl?"

"I didn't just hear about it, I saw it."

"Really?"

"Yeah! (laughing) one minute they're chatting, the next their tongues are down each other's throats and then they disappear upstairs."

"I can't believe she would do it with Brad of all people."

"Yeah, he was really bragging about it too."

"She's clearly insecure. It's a shame because she's not bad looking."

"I can't get over the fact it was Brad; everyone knows what he's like. What was she thinking?"

"Mind you, did you see what happened to Josh Hanger?"

"I heard he got knocked out."

"Yeah, it was that Vince guy who plays in the football team."

"It was pretty funny. Hanger went up to him asking for a fight, but Vincent wasn't having any of it, one punch to the chin and Hanger was on the floor."

"Wish I'd been there to see it."

"Yeah, it was great, but Vince can't go around hitting people; or he's going to end up in trouble."

"Doesn't he hang around with that Emma girl?"

"Yeah, she was off her face. She just wouldn't shut up and was being a right pain."

"She came over to me too and wouldn't leave me alone."

"Yeah, we don't really need to know how much coke she can get up her nose." The group laughed. They continued to make further jokes about the night and poke fun at each other.

Diane Deacon had heard enough and walked away. She had listened to her friends' accounts of the night but did not join in. There was no way she was going to discuss with anyone what had happened to her at the party. When she had woken up at the house, several hours later, she realised straight away that something bad had happened to her. She felt abused and traumatised.

The four friends had walked away from the party that night as very different people. Some of them had left victims in their wake, or had allowed themselves to be used, and those who had witnessed their behaviour now had a low opinion of them. Worst of all, they had set themselves up for a future that none of them wanted.

A person should always respect themselves and insist on receiving respect from others. A life of violence will not go unpunished. Someone who thinks that there is no downside to drugs will find out that there certainly is. Sexual crimes create suffering for everyone involved.

The four friends' lives were now very much on the wrong track.

Mrs Reason sat on her desk. Sometimes it was as well to be in a position to see the faces of all of her pupils and, therefore, able to gauge their reactions. As she addressed the class, she studiously cast her gaze over them all.

"We've seen how the home lives of the characters in the book have affected them, and we've now seen how they've reacted to it. Anger has led to anger, whereas a lack of affection has led to the pursuit of affection where there is none. Not being able to talk to someone about mental health issues has led to a form of self-abuse, and being the victim of a sexual crime has led to being the perpetrator of a sexual crime." She stressed her next point. "However, it is really important to realise that people react differently to different situations. Their lives could go in several directions. The boy who's suffering sexual abuse could turn to drugs or the girl whose parents argue in front of her could become violent. There are a number of ways people can turn out after suffering a dysfunctional home life. They, too, could become ineffective parents or they might turn to a life of crime. They might lack the motivation to find a job and drift into poverty or they might develop an eating disorder, such as anorexia or bulimia. All of these things can affect them or other people."

Mrs Reason wanted to make it clear that her next point was not a criticism, but instead a statement of compassion. She did not want to alienate any of her pupils, so she approached the next subject with careful professionalism.

"Remember, though, these people are victims," she said sympathetically. "Yes, some of them might do things that are awful, not just to others, but to themselves too, but you must bear in mind that they have been hurt first which is why they are becoming who they are." She made a gesture with her hands to show that what she was about to say applied to everyone. "You all know people like the characters in the book. The school bully was probably a victim first. The girl who wants sexual attention from boys might have been ignored by those closest to her. A person who is not capable of socialising likely has not had anyone to talk to. These are all people who have experienced discomfort or pain, and that fact can't be ignored."

Mrs Reason slid off the desk. She wanted her pupils to focus on themselves, rather than her. "Take a moment to think what it would be like if you were one of the characters in the book. Imagine how it would feel to experience their pain. How would it affect you? What sort of person would you become? Some of you have probably already started to draw parallels between your own lives and the characters. The question is; what decisions are you making?" She paused for a long while to give the pupils in the class some time to consider what she had just said. "The book now moves forward many years in time. All four of the main characters have become adults. What we're going to see next is how their choices lead to consequences. From this point on we will see what they have become, and more importantly, what any of you could become."

Chapter 5

Many years had passed and many bad decisions had been made by the four friends since the day of the party. Some were deliberate, whereas others were unintentional. Nevertheless, people paid a price, whether it was the perpetrators or the victims. The pain spread like a wildfire.

When they left school, Leanne, Oliver, Vincent and Emma all pretty much went their separate ways in life. They kept in touch, sometimes. A phone call occasionally came out of nowhere, which would lead to a couple of them meeting for a catch up. The foundation of their relationship had crumbled over time, but that was to be expected considering what they were all going through.

Each of them carried their own burdens. Everything their parents had done, or not done, continued to have an affect on their lives. What suffering they had experienced they passed on to others or continued to inflict on themselves. The pain was perpetual and premeditated.

Even if someone has hurt you many times through life, once they have stopped, you should never keep hurting yourself on their behalf. It is extremely hard to break away from what you have experienced, because it shapes who you have become, but sometimes you owe it to yourself to set yourself free from your past. Sometimes, however, this is easier said than done.

Oliver sat with a contented look on his face. He was relaxed and felt comfortable in his surroundings. Spending his time people watching was one of his favourite pastimes. It never involved him making any direct contact with others, but he enjoyed observing.

Now in his late twenties, Oliver had aged enough to have lost his boyhood looks, but was still thin and somewhat frail. His clothes hung loosely on him and his demeanour appeared to be one of a weak and harmless individual. If you passed him in the street you would not give him a second glance, let alone be wary of him. Nothing about him seemed threatening.

As the children dived into the water, Oliver sat in the viewing gallery discretely tapping the camera on his phone. One after the other, each moment was captured with perfect timing. With such subtlety he assumed that no one would notice, but he was wrong.

The police had been called fifteen minutes earlier. They stood in a doorway while a member of the swimming pool staff pointed at the suspect. After taking a moment to witness the perpetrator's actions for themselves they made their move.

"Excuse me, sir." The first police officer approached from the left. "We would like to ask you a few questions."

"What?" Oliver was startled. "Why?"

"If you could come with us please, sir, it would be appreciated." The second police officer was now standing directly behind and his voice turned stern. "Now!"

As Oliver stood up he tried to slip his phone under the seat. He knew that if the images were found he would be in deep trouble. It was to no avail though and his actions had been observed.

The first police officer stepped forward and picked the phone up off the floor. Oliver's shoulders slumped as he realised he had been snared, and he tried to lie his way out of the situation.

"That's not mine. I don't know whose phone that is." He ran his fingers through his hair and blinked repeatedly. "I didn't even see it there."

"You can explain everything at the police station." The second police officer pulled out a pair of handcuffs. "In the meantime, we can take a look at the images on your phone."

At that, Oliver was led away. As he was escorted out of the swimming pool a number of people watched and wondered what was going on. Some of them even guessed correctly. His humiliation was both demoralising and deserved.

A matter of hours later, Oliver learnt that the police had searched his flat and found his laptop. At this point he knew he had been caught. They would certainly find all of the other images that he had taken or downloaded. He had no choice but to confess to his actions.

Oliver had been a pervert for some years. Whether it was spying on children in parks and swimming pools, or downloading porn from the internet, his mind had sunk deeper into depravity. There had even been times when he had deliberately brushed against women's breasts and posteriors in public places, just to be sickeningly turned on by it. He had never been caught out, until now.

Since he had got away with sexually assaulting Diane Deacon at the party when he was young he assumed that he would never be caught carrying out such vile acts. Had he been discovered at the time he would probably have attended counselling and been punished in order to change his ways. Unfortunately, he had got away with it and that was the worst thing that could have happened for everyone, including him.

It had started sporadically, but soon become more and more frequent. The risks that Oliver had taken through the years had grown greater with each contemptible act. A leering stare aimed in between an unsuspecting woman's legs across a restaurant eventually led to taking a photo from the same angle. All of this had regrettably been undetected and unpunished, which in turn had meant that the regularity and magnitude of his deeds had increased.

Although Oliver had been a victim at first, he had now become the sick pervert that his father was. He had not spoken to Brian in years because of the abuse he had suffered at his hands, but he had become an exact copy of him. Whereas, when he was young and being abused it was never in his control, now he was in command of everything.

In Oliver's own mind he had gone from being the powerless to the powerful. It was all about the pursuit of control over another person. He revelled in his victim's inability to stop him and exalted in his own dominance to take from them what was not his to have. Whether it was a photo or a quick feel, he snatched from his prey what no person has the right to steal.

Oliver knew he was sick. He was aware that the acts of degradation he was committing were the vilest that a person could commit. In spite of this, he slept well at night. His conscience was not exactly clear, but he could live with his actions because he had never had to face the consequences. Quite simply, he saw no reason why he should change his disgusting ways, because it had never affected him in a negative way. Until now!

When the court case came around, Oliver pleaded guilty. It was obvious that he had no choice. There was no way he could plausibly deny what he had done and he could certainly not offer a reasonable excuse. The only question that remained was how he was going to be punished.

The judge took into consideration that it was the first time Oliver had been prosecuted for an offence, although his crimes had going undetected for years. The court was also unaware he had made physical contact with any of his victims, and so that also went in his favour. With his expressed regret and remorse for his actions, a light sentence was handed down. The final punishment was a suspended two-year prison term, one hundred hours of community service, twelve months of counselling and put on the Sex Offenders Register.

Oliver was satisfied with the sentence that had been handed down. He had pleaded guilty and confessed to his crimes, and was convinced he was going to get a custodial sentence. As he left the courtroom it seemed as though his ordeal was over with and he could finally get on with his life. However, that was not to be the case.

"This is for you." A shadowy figure stepped out of nowhere and passed an envelope to him. "You will need to read everything and fill in all the forms."

Oliver kept his hands down by his sides and did not take what he was being offered. "What is it?"

The court clerk explained. "These are the dates and places where you need to go to for your counselling and probation." He shook the envelope to encourage Oliver to take it. "There are also a number of forms that you have to sign to agree to the terms of your sentence."

Oliver reluctantly took the paperwork, but did not say anything in return. Instead, he stood there and waited for the awkward moment to pass.

"Read everything, sign everything and don't be late." The court clerk said in a cold voice. "Failure to do any of these things will result in your coming back to the court and facing a custodial sentence." At which point he turned and left.

Oliver remained behind with a sullen expression on his face. He briefly looked at the envelope, but did not open it. His ordeal was clearly not over and would last for quite some time. It seemed as though he had not got off as lightly as he had, at first, thought.

The eleventh bottle of beer went down as easily as the first. A whole day of drinking had carried on into the early evening and was starting to take its toll. Tipsy had become merry, which had then turned to drunk. Absolutely wasted was the desired end result.

Vincent was sitting at the end of the bar, half-cut and alone. The pub that he was in was not particularly popular and was normally only frequented by the more luckless members of society due to its low prices. There were a couple of scruffy looking men sitting by the entrance, a man and his dog at a table by the toilets and a barmaid who was cleaning the glasses, but other than that the place was virtually deserted. Only misplaced souls were to be found here.

Vincent had lost his job eight months previously and had been struggling to find regular employment ever since. He had been evicted from his flat and forced to move into a meagre and unfurnished bedsit in a rundown part of town. So, for some time now, his address had invariably been the corner of the bar, next to the beer taps, in the local pub.

Although Vincent did not regularly play sport as he used to at school he had kept his large physique. He had lost the muscle that he once had and could now really only be described as stocky, although his bulky stature was still overbearing. With his scowling face and steely eyes, he was not the type of person to get on the wrong side of.

Ever since Vincent had hit Josh Hanger at the party, when they were in their teens, his life had revolved around fighting. He liked nothing more than to recount the tale of how he had knocked out his boyhood nemesis with one punch and had also picked up a number of new stories to tell along the way. A few more fights at school, a road rage incident and a handful of bar scuffles had all added to his repertoire of boastful brawl stories. Quite simply, he had become a thug and a bully.

It didn't take much for Vincent to lose his temper. A brush against his shoulder in a crowded place, having to queue too long in a supermarket or someone not letting him in if he was trying to join a main road from a side street while driving, would all be enough for him to break into a rage. He justified his irate temperament by declaring that he did not take any crap from anyone but, in truth, he caused most of his altercations. There never seemed to be a reason behind any of it, and had never got his comeuppance, so he continued to behave aggressively.

Most of Vincent's victims would back off. His large physique was a daunting sight. The people who did retaliate were usually punched without hesitation, even if they only responded verbally. However, if Vincent came across someone too big or there were too many of them he would overlook the imagined infringement and let it pass. He knew his own limitations, just as he knew when someone else was scared or vulnerable. Knowing who you can get away with hitting and who you cannot is all part of being a bully.

It was no surprise that Vincent was sitting by himself. He had few friends and those that he did have were currently at work. Most of the people he had socialised with over the years either did not like him straight away or grew to detest him the more they got to know him. When it came to first impressions his moody nature always came to the fore, and this was deliberate.

The barmaid held up a bottle and forced a well-rehearsed smile on to her face. "Do you want another beer?"

"Yeah," Vincent replied sullenly, with a surly expression.

"That will be three-fifty please." The response was professionally jovial.

Vincent pushed a note across the bar. It was picked up, put in the till and then replaced with the correct change.

"Thank you."

Vincent did not know the barmaid's name. He had never bothered to find out. Even though she was always polite to him, he had never returned the effort. The only reason he went to that particular pub was for the cheap drink and certainly not to socialise with the staff, even though this one seemed pleasant enough.

Barbara had been working as a barmaid for well over two decades now. Although she had only been working at this particular pub for a little under a year, she had not taken long to learn how it was run and become familiar with the locals. Being popular with the patrons and efficient at her job were a good combination. It was no surprise when the owner offered her the role of bar manager after just six months.

At forty years old, Barbara had experienced enough in life to know how to interact with people and handle difficult customers. She had got being a barmaid in a low rent establishment down to an art. She dressed appropriately for the job, but never looked cheap. If the conversation was low brow she would be cheeky, whereas if the discussion was intelligent she could raise her game. When a patron wanted to talk to her she would always be friendly, but she could tell which customers wanted to be left alone. Barbara was an astute people person who knew how to deal with everyone who entered the premises.

As the door to the pub opened, sounds from the street outside flooded in, but were immediately drowned out by the two drunken men who lurched inside. The few people in the bar glanced round at them and then went back to whatever they were doing. It was obvious the men were intoxicated and had spent several hours drinking to get to the state that they were in. Although they were talking loudly to each other, they seemed jovial and were spontaneously making each other laugh.

One of the inebriated men was tall and skinny, whereas the other was short and stocky. They were both wearing suits, with crooked ties, and appeared to be office workers who had strayed from the centre of town. Neither of them looked older than their late twenties and they seemed harmless, even if they were being a bit too loud.

The taller of the two men staggered over to the bar, leant up against it and placed his order for drinks. In most pubs anyone who was too drunk would not be served, but this drinking establishment was known for being liberal. His friend came across to join him and they stood there unsteadily waiting for their drinks. It was not long before they were served and their boisterousness continued.

The shorter of the two men started the banter. "Why didn't you get a suit that fits you? I've seen giraffes with tighter fitting clothes."

The response was just as cutting. "You should've got a hat with yours. It might have made you over four feet tall."

Neither took offence and they both laughed loudly at themselves and each other. This backwards and forwards mockery carried on for some time, with both of them laughing louder with each insult, until things took a turn in the wrong direction.

The short man made a joke aimed at his mate, so the taller one pushed him away, but only in a playful manner. This would have been quite harmless but, due to the large amount of alcohol that the stocky man had consumed, he lost his balance and stumbled backwards. He managed to stop himself from falling to the floor, but accidently knocked against the man who was sitting at the bar behind him.

Vincent reacted immediately. "Hey! What are doing?" His voice was loud and angry. "Get the hell off me!"

"Sorry, pal." The short man raised his hands in a submissive gesture. "I lost my balance."

Despite being very drunk, his friend could see that a situation was arising and tried to make amends. "Hey, that was my fault. I pushed him. Sorry about that."

Vincent was not about to accept their apologies. He stood up, instinctively clenching his fists. His chest expanded and he stood up on his toes to make himself appear bigger.

"Are you trying to start something?" He glared at each of them in turn. "Do you think you're hard?"

"Hey, we don't want a fight."

"We don't want any trouble, dude."

That was the worst thing they could have said. They had revealed that they were not the type to fight back. Vincent now knew if punches were thrown no blows would be swung in the opposite direction. This would be a one-way fight.

Vincent knew easy victims when he saw them. These two were clearly not the brawling type and, to make things even easier, they were visibly drunk. The expression on both of their faces was anxious to the point of fear. This interaction would not be on equal terms.

At times like these, Vincent had something akin to a checklist to warrant a dispute. One of them had deliberately knocked into him, so they had started it. Both of them were clearly trying to gang up on him, so that would be self-defence. Finally, the two of them were still there, so they obviously wanted a fight. The entire conflict was undoubtedly all their own doing.

As much as Vincent was ready to lash out, he was cautious of any repercussions. For all he knew, one of them could have been trained in martial arts or be an amateur boxer. He made one last test to see if they were willing to retaliate.

Vincent took a step forward and raised his fist. This would mean one of two things. If the response was a raised guard, like a trained fighter, it would be time to back down. However, if the faces remained frightened and arms stayed down by their sides this meant there would be no attempt to block a punch and no counterattack either. In this case the latter applied.

The first blow hit the tallest one on the side of the jaw, instantly knocking him to the floor. Getting the biggest bloke out of the way first was always a good strategy. As for the second punch, that landed on the nose of the second man, sending blood spraying from his nostrils. A few more strikes came in the way of swings and kicks just to teach them a lesson. The fight was one-sided, had two victims and zero point to it.

There had been little reaction from the rest of the people in the pub and they had watched the fight without any motivation to get involved. Even Barbara stayed out of it, which was understandable. She was a barmaid, not a bouncer.

Vincent towered over the two men who were both now lying on the floor. His face was twisted with rage and his fists were tightly clenched. This was real anger, but it was very much self-fabricated. The two drunks had not done anything to make him this furious; it was just how he liked to be.

Barbara realised that the incident had ended. She slowly and calmly walked across to Vincent, being careful not to get too close. She spoke in a mild manner and her words were carefully chosen. "You better leave now." She motioned towards the door. "The police will be here soon."

This was not a threat, it was a warning; to appear as though the perpetrator might end up in trouble, when it was actually to get him off the premises.

Vincent was not stupid, even if he was rather primitive in his actions. He knew that he would be in a lot of trouble if he was arrested for assault. As much as he would claim that it was self-defence, he knew this would not stand up in a court. He realised it was time to leave.

Vincent strutted over to the bar indifferently, grabbed his coat and made for the door. He turned to take one last look at his victims, sneered and then left. Behind him he left blood, bruises and bewilderment.

When Vincent had got about two streets away from the bar a police car sped past him in the direction he had come from. He smiled to himself and did not even glance back; convinced he had got away with what he had just done.

Three spiders crawled down the wall. They were all exactly the same size and in a perfect line. It was almost unnatural how similar they were to each other and how neatly they seemed to be in a column. This could not be real.

Emma's winced at the sight of the spiders. She turned away for a moment in the hope they might disperse, but when she looked back they were still there. These were the worst kinds of hallucinations. The ones she knew were not real, but they remained entrenched in her mind regardless.

In a moment of exasperation, Emma glanced around the office. Even though no one was aware of what she was visualising she still did not want anyone to know that she was in such a stressed state. It was very embarrassing for her to be so out of control of her own thoughts and she would never be able to explain it to anyone even if she had wanted to. She would have to suffer alone and in silence, as she always did.

Emma had been working in the city for a number of years now. She had managed to get her foot in the door in the human resources department of an investment bank. She was good with people and enjoyed the day-to-day interaction with the other staff members. On occasion, she would interview prospective employees and play a part in the decision of whether to offer them a place in the company. She liked the challenge of figuring out people. However, even though she enjoyed her job, she felt she was capable of achieving much more.

Prior to her employment, Emma had only just advanced her way through college. She had left with enough qualifications to earn a reasonable wage, but had not really fulfilled her academic potential. The option of higher education had appealed to her, but she needed money.

Ever since Emma had first tried cocaine it had been a major part of her life. It had begun as a casual way of enjoying a night out. After that, it had become a more recreational pursuit every time she socialised. That had then turned into a habit that sucked up the majority of her wages. All of this had certainly come at a cost.

Emma had picked up a number of scars over the years, both physical and mental. Whether she self-harmed with her fingernails or the inhalation of drugs it invariably left a mark. She wore long sleeves or bangles to cover the scars on her arms, and a smile on her face to conceal the wounds in her mind. Inflicting either pain or pleasure upon herself was the only way she knew how to suppress her mental health problems. On this occasion she would choose the solace of bliss.

Whenever Emma was suffering from hallucinations the most efficient remedy she knew was to take drugs. The option of talking to someone about her problems had never been available to her and, as she wasn't willing to discuss them with anyone, it never would be either. Therefore, her only option to deal with her visions was to counteract them by turning to an equally artificial lift. Cocaine was a synthetic solution to a real problem.

Feeling the need to suppress the demons in her mind, Emma decided that she should turn to the devil. She stood up from her chair and glanced around the office. No one seemed to be paying any attention to her, so she slipped off to the toilets. Just a small pick-me-up would suffice.

As Emma entered the restroom she checked each cubicle to make sure no one was there. When she was satisfied that she was alone she went into the end stall and closed the door behind her. It was not long before she was feverishly shuffling through her handbag looking for her dose of futile first aid. A couple of minutes later the toxic medication was prepared. There on the toilet cistern was a line of cocaine, ready to be inhaled.

Emma rolled up a banknote and leant over ready to administer the dose. Soon the torment in her head would be replaced by the welcome bliss that the drug provided. Pain would turn to pleasure and, more importantly, the haunting hallucinations would be replaced with more pleasant images. This would provide relief, if only for a short time.

As she was about to suck up the white powder from the top of the cistern, Emma heard a noise behind her. She looked up and, much to her horror, saw her manager with two members of the board of directors. In her haste, she had closed the door behind her, but had forgotten to lock it. She had been caught red-handed.

Neither of the directors said anything. Emma was speechless too. It was left to her manager to break the silence. "I need to see you in my office please, Emma."

Nothing else needed to be said. The manager turned and left, with the two directors following close behind. That had certainly not been expected by any of them.

Emma was left alone. She glanced at the cocaine and then back to the door. Within a few seconds the line was gone and she was wiping her nose.

"It was not mine. Someone else must have put it there." Emma tried to lie herself out of trouble. "Honestly, I was bending over looking at it. I wondered what it was."

"You're fired." The response was blunt, but said in a calm manner. "I'm sorry, Emma, but I can't keep you on under the circumstances. The company has a zero-tolerance policy when it comes to drugs. There is no negotiating. I have to terminate your employment."

Tamsin had been the manager of the human resources department at the investment bank for more than a decade. She was efficient at her job and considered worthy of progressing to an executive position in the not too distant future. Although she was only in her mid-thirties she was climbing the corporate ladder fast in this very large company. It was not her intention to languish in the human resources department and she had made that clear to the directors.

As far as supervising people, Tamsin treated everyone with respect and would talk to those below her in the company in the same way that she did those above her. The cleaner and the managing director were both greeted on first name terms every day. For this approach she was well-liked and highly thought of by everyone.

Most people would consider Tamsin to be a 'power woman'. She always wore a suit to work which gave her a professional, but stylish appearance. Her physique was toned from spending hours in the gym every week. Success was something she strived for outside of office hours to an equal degree. Everything about her indicated that she knew what she wanted and nothing was going to stop her from getting it. However, as much as she was self-driven, she knew the value of having respect for others.

"You know it's nothing personal, Emma. I like you. We roomed together on the equal opportunities course last year. It was good spending time with you." Tamsin's smile turned to a frown. "But everyone knows you're on coke."

"What?" Emma tried to deny the accusation. "But I am not. Why would anyone think that?"

"Do you think people don't notice when we go for drinks at the bar in Docklands? They see the change in your behaviour. And there's the backwards and forwards to the toilets. It all adds up." Tamsin shook her head in a regretful manner. "I never thought you'd do it at work though. If I had known it was that bad I would have said something to you. I would have tried to help."

"I don't need help. I really don't…"

"Emma, you've just been caught sniffing cocaine in the office toilets at ten-forty in the morning." Tamsin leant forward and rested her hands on the table. "You need help. You really do."

Emma did not want to hear any more. Even though she was being forced to acknowledge the facts, she did not want to face the bitter truth. She would rather just get this over and done with and get the hell out of there. The situation was embarrassing, degrading and far too self-appraising. She did not like it at all.

With her fate sealed, Emma finally accepted the inevitable. "So that's it then. I don't even get any notice?"

"No. Sorry."

Emma sat with her head bowed. She was as much humiliated as she was downcast. This was the first time she had been sacked. Even though she knew that she had overstepped the mark and it was all her own fault, she could not help feeling sorry for herself. A tear rolled down her cheek.

Tamsin could see that the situation was becoming more awkward than it needed to be. Although she could not reverse her decision she did not want to see the young woman in front of her completely fall from grace. It was not in her nature to watch a person suffering without offering at least some hope if she was able to do so. She opened the top drawer of her desk and pulled out a business card.

"Take this. It's the phone number of a drugs counsellor I know." Tamsin quickly spoke again to prevent being interrupted. "He's very good and won't judge you. His name is Ryan."

Emma paused for a moment and then took the business card. She realised the meeting was over and stood up to leave. As she reached the door she looked back

"What makes you think I need counselling?" she asked forlornly.

"Well, I did when I was in your position." Tamsin sat back in her chair and folded her arms. "Why the hell do you think I have a drugs counsellor's card in my top drawer?"

Emma was shocked. She knew Tamsin was a highly driven individual. There was no way she could imagine this strong-minded woman in a moment of weakness. All she could do was nod in acknowledgement. With the meeting terminated, along with her employment, Emma left.

As the fingers tapped in the phone number, a light drizzle of rain splashed against the screen of the phone. It took a while for it to start ringing and when it did the handset was raised to the ear. Emma then spoke in a calm, but timid voice. "Hello! I'd like to speak to Ryan please."

The nightclub was packed. Clubbers danced wildly, drank enthusiastically or did both to excess. Most of those present were dressed to create an impression. Women showed off their newest black dress and expensive haircuts, whereas the men wore the latest fashion in shirts, trousers and shoes. Everyone was out to be seen, with the intention of attracting attention.

This particular club had a reputation as a place to go to meet potential partners. Its name, 'Promiscuous', gave an indication of what went on there. Groups of men stood around eyeing up women, and the women were checking out the men. This was a place where singles became couples and couples became single.

Of all the local nightclubs this was Leanne's favourite. She would regularly visit with friends or, sometimes, on her own if no one else could make it. Whether she came in a group or alone she would invariably leave as one half of a twosome. There was no other way that she would want to spend the night.

Leanne had been to a lot of other nightspots around the town, but had decided that they were not to her liking. After a few months, she had found that the people in them were idiots and jerks. At least that's what she told herself.

It had not taken long for Leanne to earn herself a reputation in the local clubbing scene. She would visit a place for a while, meet a different man every week and be recognised every time she went back there. The gossip was always the same.

"There's that girl from last week."

"Isn't she the one who Dave and Pete have had?"

Even the other women would make sly comments.

"Look who's come back for more."

"You think she'd have more self-respect."

"She wants to be careful she doesn't catch something."

It would, eventually, become obvious to Leanne what people were saying about her. She would notice them gesturing towards her and whispering. The feeling of being judged made her feel awful, so she would find another place to go where other clubbers did not recognise her. Leanne always blamed the place and the people, but sooner or later, whichever club she visited, it ended in with the same gossiping and finger pointing.

Leanne was not the only girl to have one-night stands. Many others did too. She just made it so easy for the men she chose. Sometimes, they did not even have to approach her and instead she made all the effort. There had even been times she had seen a man she liked the look of and walked straight up to him to ask if he wanted to come back to hers. It was as easy and simple as that.

In truth, Leanne wanted to be loved. In fact, that was all she needed. Unfortunately, she was going completely the wrong way about getting the attention she craved. She told herself that the men in her life were really impressed by her, but if that was the case why did she inevitably end up on her own again. What she wanted was affection, but as she only ever asked for sex, that was all she got.

Leanne walked around the club, searching for someone who might quench her lustful desires. There were tall men, muscular men, smart men and short men. They all had their own appeal, but none of them seemed to have that little bit of extra special something she wanted. None of the men that she had observed appeared to be risky or dangerous enough. It seemed as though she was going to draw a blank tonight, until she saw him.

He was not particularly tall, not that muscular, hardly stylish and just attractive enough, but he was certainly confident. He moved and conducted himself in a very self-assured way. He swaggered to the bar and leant up against it like he owned it. This was a man who did not just think he was the best; he was absolutely certain of it. Unfortunately, for Leanne she was not what he was looking for.

One after the other, the man spoke to every woman he cast his eye on. Tall women, short women, blonde, brunette…whatever he liked the look of. Not one of them was out of his sights. However, none of them seemed interested.

Leanne watched his every move, dumfounded as to why none of the women he spoke to seemed get to first base. He seemed to be interested in them, but none of them responded to his advances. It was quite perplexing.

As the night went on it appeared that the object of Leanne's desire would never notice her. She had walked past him on a number of occasions while he was talking to other women and had sent a few smiles his way. At one point she even deliberately bumped into him and apologised. He acknowledged her briefly, but carried on talking to the woman next to him. It appeared no amount of flirting was going to work. Leanne decided it was time to give up. She would finish her drink and make her way home.

"Hi," said a voice beside her.

Leanne had been standing at the bar, peering into her half-empty glass. She immediately looked up to see who had spoken. It was him.

"I've got to say, you've caught my eye," he continued with polished confidence. He eyed her up and down. "I like what I see."

Bruno did not have a single wrinkle in his impeccably ironed clothes nor was there a hair out of place on his head. His shoes were so shiny that only his necklace and rings glistened more in the colourful nightclub lights. He had obviously spent a lot of time getting ready; however, it was not to please anyone else other than himself. The effort would always be worth it if he achieved his goal.

As Bruno reeled off his usual chat-up lines the expression on his face said he was doing Leanne a favour just by talking to her. Even when he offered her a drink it was as though he was giving her a priceless gift. His self-assuredness knew no limits, but he was not the only one out for themselves.

Leanne was ecstatic. She felt like she was the most sought-after person in the club. In her eyes all the other women had failed to catch the big fish, but now she was going to reel him in. There was no way she was going to let this one get away. It was just a matter of giving him what he wanted to make sure he did not slip from her grasp.

What remained of the conversation was as frivolous as it was unnecessary. They both knew what it was paving the way to. The swapping of names was less important than whose house they were going to. Any chat from this point on was merely to give the impression that they were interested in each other's personality, though they were plainly not. When they finally decided to leave together it was inevitable, like a train arriving at its destination.

When Leanne opened her eyes, she realised straightaway she was in a place she had never been before. This was not new to her. It would not take long for her to get her bearings and everything from the night before to come rushing back, which it did. A smile crossed her face.

Leanne could hear the sound of running water coming through the open door. She guessed that Bruno must be in the shower, as there was no one in the bed next to her. Wearing only her underwear, she got up and made her way out on to the landing. It was at this point she realised she was not alone.

A middle-aged woman was standing in a doorway to another bedroom, staring directly at Leanne. Her expression was both scrutinising and stern. Her arms were tightly crossed against her chest and she certainly did not give off the impression of being welcoming. In fact, quite the opposite.

Leanne immediately felt uncomfortable and put her arms over her breasts to cover what flesh she could, feeling embarrassed. Her partial nudity made the situation even more awkward. In an effort to ease the situation she found herself in she made an attempt at a greeting.

"Hi!" It was all she could think of.

The woman barely nodded in return and did not raise a smile. She turned around and went back into her bedroom. As she closed the door behind her it was just possible to see her briefly shake her head.

That was clearly Bruno's mother and she did not appear to be too pleased. Whether it was the young woman she found on her landing or the behaviour of her son that had irritated her was not at all apparent. Either way, she had not tried to hide her feelings. In fact, Leanne was glad she did not have to attempt further conversation with her, but that would all change in the not too distant future.

Chapter 6

The pub was about half full, which meant there were far more customers than usual. Although music was playing and most people were talking it was quiet enough to have a conversation, which was just as well, as someone had something to say to a certain individual.

Vincent walked through the door from the street and immediately caught the eye of the person who had been looking out for him. As he made his way to the bar he was closely watched by the onlooker.

"I'll have a beer," he said, on arrival at the bar.

There was no reply. The barmaid stared silently at Vincent. This was not to his liking.

"I'll have a beer," he repeated.

Still there was no response.

"Is there a problem?" Vincent looked vexed.

"I need to talk to you," Barbara said finally, after a long pause.

Barbara was not someone Vincent had punched or bullied, neither was she a relative or a friend of such a person. She had not yet stated what it was she wanted to talk about, but it was quite obvious. Vincent knew the recent fight was going to be the topic of conversation. He would never have allowed this normally, but on this occasion he had no choice. There was no way he was going to get a beer otherwise.

Barbara stood behind the bar eyeing Vincent with an unimpressed expression on her face. Her demeanour was one of someone who clearly had a point to make and nothing was going to stop her from making it. This was a woman who meant business.

Although Barbara had aged well she had a face that suggested she had endured more than her fair share of life's blows. There seemed to be a slight, but permanent scowl etched on her face and her tight lips appeared as though they could only muster the faintest of smiles. She was certainly someone who gave the impression of having endured a lot of hardship through the years and was not about to take any more.

As bar manager, it was up to Barbara who drank in the pub and who did not. She had the final say over whether someone was barred, just as it was her decision whether someone would be served if they had drunk too much. She opened the conversation with Vincent in her usual calm and measured way.

"I know I don't have to tell you what this is about." She motioned her hand towards a small table with two chairs next to it in the corner of the pub. "Let's take a seat."

"No, it's OK thanks." Vincent spoke in a curt manner. "I'll stand here."

"Well, I'm going to sit over there anyway. Whether you join me or not is up to you, but no one else in this bar is going to serve you but me. It's your decision." She then walked across to the table and sat down with a glass of water.

Vincent peered around the bar. There was only one other barmaid working. She was only young, so he had a pretty good idea that she would have been given orders not to serve him. He reluctantly conceded that he had no choice but to do as he was requested, although it felt more like a demand than an invitation.

Vincent sat down and slouched in the chair, folding his arms in a dismissive posture. He wanted to get this over and done with as soon as possible. It was his intention to nod his head a few times, agree to tone down his behaviour and then get on with drinking.

Barbara, however, had other plans. She knew that the young man before her would humour her and make empty assurances to control his unruly conduct. She did not plan to let him treat her like a fool. She spoke in a precise and composed manner.

"I'm not going to waste your time or mine with the usual nonsense about not arguing with the other customers. It's obvious that you don't care about that. I'm clearly not going to bar you either. I would've done that the moment you walked through the door if that was my intention." Barbara leant forward. "I'm also not going to tell you that I have reported you to the police. They came, but I said I didn't recognise you."

This was a relief to Vincent, and it showed as he uncrossed his arms and relaxed into a less rigid position. The fact that he could face charges for assault had been clawing at the back of his mind recently and he had actually been concerned about the consequences. With this knowledge in mind a smile crossed his face. However, he was not so in the clear as he thought.

"I do, however, want to talk to you about what you did."

Vincent was not about to accept this. There was no way he was going to take a reprimand from anyone, even if it meant not getting served a beer or being barred.

"There's absolutely no way you're going to sit there and give me a sermon." Vincent sat up straight in his chair and jutted out his chin. "It's just not going to happen."

"No, I'm not. I'm not your mother," Barbara replied scornfully. "Telling you off clearly didn't work when you were a kid, so I doubt it's going to work now you're an adult."

Vincent looked perplexed. The conversation was not going in the direction he thought it would. In fact, he had absolutely no idea whatsoever where it was going. Nothing became any clearer once the first question was asked.

"Do you know why I'm drinking water?" Barbara lifted her glass up into their line of sight.

"No." Vincent was puzzled.

"It's because I'm a lousy drunk. When I've had a drink I'm a complete bitch. I'm argumentative, obnoxious and an utter moron. I'm rude to strangers. In fact, I have no respect for anyone, even my own family and friends. I am the biggest waster you'll ever meet."

Barbara placed the glass back on the table. "So I choose not to drink, so as not to be that person."

"Why are you telling me this?" Vincent was starting to feel bemused.

"Because you remind me of my father. You're just like him." Barbara's voice was cold and bitter. "He was a complete bastard, and so are you!"

Vincent was taken aback by this, naturally, but, for some reason, he was not angered about being so blatantly insulted. Normally, his temper would have flared, but on this occasion it abated. As the verbal abuse kept coming he sat and listened to every word.

"I've been working this bar for years and have watched you every time you come in. You've got no respect for people. You're rude. You look for the slightest reason to get into a confrontation. Your answer to any dispute is to lose your temper. You always think you're in the right, even when you're not. Half the disturbances that take place in here involve you, and you always stroll back in afterwards like nothing happened." Barbara shook her head. "You're like my father, and I'm like him as well; a complete bitch."

Vincent could not help but respect the woman before him. She was not only criticising him, but she was also berating her own father, as well as herself. He could hardly tell her not to speak to him like that because she was also condemning her own actions. If she was willing to face the truth, then he would have to too.

"It's no wonder I became who I was. I never had a chance. People like us are normally made by people like us. My father moulded me out of his anger. He used to drink in a bar just like this and regularly came home off his face, covered in bruises. The only thing he enjoyed more than fighting was bragging about his fights. There was never any remorse for the victims. He always had a reason for it. 'I don't take any crap from anyone!' That was his favourite excuse. It was always him who started it though. I should know. When he hit my mother, sister and me, none of us had ever thrown the first punch." Barbara rubbed the side of her face as if she could still feel where she had been struck.

"It was inevitable that I would turn out the way I did. My father passed on his temper to me like a family heirloom, and when you carry something like that you pass it on as well. I got into arguments with the other kids at school, and then that carried on into adult life when I inevitably turned to alcohol. It didn't take much for me to get into a fracas with complete strangers and, like anyone that obnoxious, I fell out with my family and friends." Barbara drew an imaginary ring on the table with her finger and pointed to the middle. "You're in the centre of a circle and you fall out with everyone around you. None of the other people have a problem with each other. It's always you and someone else. You come out with the same excuses that the other person started it, even though you've heard it all before, but you're the one who gives out all the crap in the first place. It's only when you lose everything and have nothing left that you realise it's all been your fault and it's you who has to change. And, trust me, when it suddenly dawns on you that you have absolutely nothing in your life, it's the biggest smack in the mouth you will ever get. No one will hit you harder than that. Honestly, you don't want to end up where I was."

Barbara took a moment to contemplate her own words. It clearly still hurt for her to think about her past, but managed to stay remarkably composed. This was a woman who had deep scars beneath the surface.

She had Vincent's attention. He did not just want answers, he needed them. "So what happened to you?" It was an obvious question. "What brought about the change?"

Barbara took a deep breath before she answered. "I fell in love. He was a lovely man. The most kind, generous and thoughtful person you could meet. We had a child; a daughter. It was the happiest I had been in my life. I had to go and ruin it though." She closed her eyes in a futile attempt to shut out the pain, but it was still there, a permanent resident in her mind.

"I'd kept on drinking throughout the relationship, and with that regularly used to lose my temper over nothing. He always made allowances for my bad behaviour in his usual understanding way. He saw the best in everyone, especially in me, the mother of his child. 'My best was worth putting up with my worst,' he used to say. Then one day my worst became unbearable even for him. I went one step too far and my life changed forever."

Vincent had rarely been one to care about other people's problems and would never have normally entertained having to listen to such a heartfelt release of emotion, but he could not help feeling a connection to the woman opposite him. Although he had spoken to her before when ordering a drink, he had never actually had a conversation with her. If fact, he did not even know her name and was not sure whether she knew his. As she carried on speaking his attention remained fixed on her every word.

"My father was in court for sentencing. He had punched someone in a bar and they had suffered a blood clot on the brain. It could've killed them. He was lucky he wasn't on a manslaughter charge. Not that he got away with it. The judge took into consideration all of his previous offences and sent him to prison for six years. It came as a shock to all of my family, including me." Barbara raised the glass of water, took a sip and carried on. "I did my usual and hit the bottle. Within hours I was absolutely wasted. It didn't take much for me to find something to lose my temper about. Shouting, throwing things and smashing anything breakable. My partner took the brunt of it, but did his best to remain calm, until I did the unthinkable. I hit my daughter. She needed seven stitches across the forehead. A glass ashtray can be a devastating weapon."

A tear rolled down Barbara's cheek, but she did not let that stop her. "Kind, generous and thoughtful people don't like people who hit kids. The police were called and I was arrested. He got custody and I got visiting rights. From that point on I couldn't even wake up every morning and see my own daughter. Whereas once I could cuddle her every day, I could now only hold her at the weekends. I'd lost everything that I loved. I don't blame him for anything. It was all my own doing. Everything that happened was my fault."

Barbara sat up straight as if to steady herself for an impending blow. "Ten years later, my daughter hates me. She loves me, but she hates me. She knows what I've done and who I've been. She's forgiven me, but when I look her in the eye I know she remembers everything. She's still got the scar on her forehead as a reminder of who her mother is. My ex did everything right. He made sure I always had exactly the right amount of hours that I was allowed to see her. Not once did he criticise me behind my back. The perfect partner was the perfect ex, as well as the perfect father."

Vincent was not the type of person to show compassion, but he made an effort to comfort the broken soul before him. "That's really rough. It must've been hard for you."

"I'm not the same person anymore. That person who used to find answers in a neat whisky doesn't exist. The person I am now holds a glass of water and discovers the answer with a clear mind. But this conversation isn't about me. It's about you. What do you think will happen if you keep on beating people up? How do you think your life will end up?"

Although Vincent had not thought about it, it was obvious that this question was going to be asked at some point. Now that it was put before him he would have to confront it. The truth would not be comfortable, but he also couldn't lie after Barbara had been so honest with him.

"I suppose I'll end up in prison. If I get married she will end up leaving me. And If I have kids they'll hate me." The expression on his face was understandably morose as he gave his final verdict. "I'll ruin my life."

"Don't be like me. Don't screw up your life," said Barbara. "Prison is no place to spend your life, and I'm not just talking about the place where they send criminals. Your mind can be a prison as well. The walls are made of your anger, the bars are made out of your violence and the door is made of your cruelty to others. Escape that cell or you will be there for the rest of your life.

"If I can give you one piece of advice it's this: learn the word 'stop'. When you're about to do something that is going to harm someone else or you, just say 'stop'. That word might save you from the abyss one day. It could be the difference between ending up with nothing or making something of your life. There are sixty seconds in a minute, sixty minutes in an hour, twenty-four hours in a day and three hundred and sixty-five days in a year. Allow yourself just one or two of those minutes to make a decision that could affect the rest of your life. You could be on this planet for years, decades. With all that time available, you owe yourself sixty seconds. Because, if you don't, you could spend years regretting what could have and should have been."

Vincent had never felt like this before, but then he had never had someone go out of their way to help him. Suddenly, someone wanted the best for him and, not only that, they understood him. They had been through what he had and it showed him that he was not alone. It made him want to share his own past, so for the first time in his life that is what he did.

"It was my stepfather. He used to hit me. Like any boy sometimes I did something wrong, but nothing that deserved the beatings I received. Alcohol played its part. He drank heavily. That was when he was at his worst." Vincent bowed his head as a moment of shame washed over him. "I suppose I'm not much different."

"It doesn't have to be that way. People say a leopard never changes its spots, but human beings aren't leopards. We can all change if we want to." Barbara pointed to Vincent and then back at herself. "You and I have been kicked in life. We've had more than our fair share of knocks. That's led to us kicking others who also didn't deserve it. But that then comes back at us. So, whenever we hit out, we're actually kicking ourselves as well, and what makes it worse is that we're doing so on behalf of the people who used to hurt us. What makes this so ridiculous is that the people who originally hurt us have moved out of our lives. They've stopped doing it, but we're carrying it on. When someone does something stupid they say, 'I could kick myself.' Well, how stupid are we that we actually do? It's absurd and it's time for it to stop."

Vincent nodded. He understood exactly what was being said. This was his battle and the only way he could win it was to stop throwing punches. "I've got to sort myself out."

"In the same way it was me versus me, it is now you versus you." Barbara summed up. "You've been kicked enough. It's time for you to put a stop to it. Become someone new. Put the old you in the past. Hate that other person and respect the person you want to be. The time to act is now."

There was silence as the two of them gathered their thoughts. They had both said what they wanted to say and were taking a moment to let it sink in. Barbara was satisfied that her message had got across and Vincent had accepted the lesson that he had been taught. It had been beneficial to both of them. One had helped the other and, in so doing, had shed some of their own burden, whereas the other person had been helped and made to realise that they had a burden to unload. This was a moment of fulfilment for the pair of them, followed by a belated introduction.

"I'm Barbara, by the way. I think we should know each other's names considering that we know so much about each other's lives." Before the young man sitting opposite her could respond she spoke again. "And you're Vincent. I've watched you enough to know who you are."

At that, Barbara put her hand out to offer a handshake. Vincent immediately reached across the table and responded. He had never had someone talk to him like this before. It was not often that people showed him that much respect. When he spoke it was with sincerity. It's nice to meet you, Barbara." He then added something he rarely said. "Thank you."

"Who the hell is she?" Leanne shouted at the top of her voice.

"She's no one." Bruno was clearly stressed, but not apologetic. "It was only a peck on the cheek."

"You kissed her on the lips. I saw it."

"I did not. There is no way I did that. I would never do that to you."

Leanne had arrived at Bruno's house to pay him a surprise visit, but as she had got there she had seen him kissing another girl in a car parked outside. She had immediately approached them, but they had seen her coming. He had quickly jumped out of the car, and the girl had rapidly driven off. It was at this point the argument had begun.

Bruno lived in a large house with his mother in the wealthier part of town. It was not really the kind of neighbourhood where an angry shouting match would be accepted by the residents. Sculptured bushes and long driveways were the norm, not raised voices and finger pointing. Such behaviour was frowned upon.

"She just gave me a lift home. I work with her." As Bruno tried to justify his actions he made his way to the front door and hurriedly tried to unlock it. "The trains are running late again and I lost my ticket."

"But you haven't been at work today. It's Saturday." Leanne was not about to accept this weak explanation. "Yesterday you told me you were going to a friend's house."

"I got called into work this morning, at the last minute." Bruno opened the front door and quickly made his way inside. "It happens sometimes. I needed the overtime."

Leanne stepped through the doorway and stood glaring at Bruno. Her expression was angry, but also hurt. She wanted answers, but whether she wanted to hear the truth was another thing altogether.

"OK, tell me what happened right from the start. I want to know every detail."

Bruno said nothing. His mind was working frantically trying to think of an answer to excuse his actions.

"I'm out of cigarettes," he said eventually. With that, he barged past Leanne and walked through the still open front door. "I'll be back in five minutes."

At that, Bruno was gone and with him any truthful account of what had just occurred. This was quite deliberate. He found that the best way to get out of a bad situation was to get away from it. His escape had been as slick as one of his chat-up lines.

Leanne watched helplessly as Bruno swiftly made his way up the drive. She could have run after him, but she found herself rooted to the spot. It was almost as if she could not bring herself to confront him further. Whatever Bruno had said, be it truth or a lie, would not have made much difference as Leanne suspected she would have been hurt either way. Her ignorance, however, was about to be enlightened.

"You realise he's not coming back, darling." A posh voice said behind Leanne. "I think that is obvious."

Standing at the top of the stairs was Angelina, Bruno's mother. Her face showed displeasure at the loud argument that had occurred in the vicinity of her home. There was something about her, however, that suggested she was familiar with such an event and it was not the first time that she had witnessed a public falling out.

Angelina was wearing an expensive silk dressing gown that hung limply around her slender frame. Her hair was tied above her head, but still managed to look stylish. Although she was middle-aged, the years had treated her well. She had few wrinkles and her well-shaped cheekbones enhanced her face. This woman looked like she had class and the way she was so well spoken confirmed that.

"You might as well close the door and come in." Angelina glided down the stairs and headed towards the kitchen. "As you're here, I'll make you a cup of tea and we can have a chat."

Leanne watched as Angelina swept past her. She found herself stuck, not knowing quite what to do, and it was only when a gust of cold wind blew into the house that she realised she was still standing by the open doorway. Although she really did not want to stay, she closed the door behind her and followed Angelina into the kitchen. She could not help feeling a certain amount of inquisitiveness as to why Bruno's mother would want to converse with her. They had been introduced to each other months ago, but other than exchanging the occasional brief greeting, they had never really spoken to each other.

As Leanne entered the kitchen she put her bag on the worktop and sat down on one of the tall stools that were neatly placed around it. She did not say anything but her glum expression, tinged with anger, expressed her mood. Part of her wanted to scream, but she also wanted to roll up into a ball and disappear for good.

Angelina put the kettle on and it quickly heated up. She then dropped a couple of teabags into an ornate teapot and set out two matching cups. It looked like a formal tea party, but when Angelina began to speak the conversation was anything but.

"I assume you caught my son with another girl? I could hear the commotion from upstairs. Heaven knows what the neighbours must think." Angelina poured boiled water from the kettle into the teapot. "You're not the first one to catch him out and you probably won't be the last."

"Really!" A look of disgust crossed Leanne's face. "He's done it before?"

"Of course he has, darling. Surely this doesn't surprise you?"

"It does."

"Well, it shouldn't." Angelina spoke like it was the most obvious thing in the world. "He cheats on all his girlfriends. You must have realised he's the type to do that?"

"No, I didn't." Leanne was surprised, not just about what she was hearing, but the source of the news. "I had no idea that he would do something like that."

Angelina started to pour the tea into each cup alternatively. "You mean to say you had no idea that he's a cheater?"

"No. I didn't have a clue."

"Then you've not been honest with yourself."

"Sorry…"

"You are deluded."

Leanne was not impressed. She had been brought up to respect her elders but was finding it difficult to be spoken to so frankly by a woman she barely knew.

"I am not deluded." She lifted her chin defiantly. "And I don't like the way you're talking to me."

Angelina smiled and pushed a cup of steaming tea towards Leanne. She calmly took a sip of her own drink before placing the cup back on the worktop.

"Darling, everyone lies to themselves and others. In fact, honest people admit they lie, whereas dishonest people say they don't." She crossed her legs and rested her hands on her knee. "Which are you?"

Leanne was taken aback. There was a lot of truth in what she had just heard. She told lies. She just did not like to admit it. Although she wanted to come back with a defence she could not think of anything to say.

Angelina did not want to humiliate the young woman in front of her, especially after what she had been through. It was not her intention to make things worse, quite the opposite.

She did not want to see someone so callously wounded, particularly at the hands of her own son. With this in mind she continued carefully.

"Think back to how Bruno behaved when you first met him. Surely you picked up on his arrogance, his pre-planned words, and the fact that he made you feel great about yourself. You must have worked out that everything was well-practised and acted out like a play. Did it not occur to you that you might not be the only woman on this earth he felt an immediate attraction to?"

This all made sense to Leanne. She had been completely won over by Bruno within seconds of meeting him. Now that she thought about it, the fact that she had been so enthralled by him was all her own doing. She had intended to be swept off her feet and her compliance did not even have to be earned. As she acknowledged her misjudgement she felt embarrassed and meek.

"I suppose he was a bit full of himself. It was obvious he was just out to have fun. He tried it on with enough other girls before he even got to me." Leanne took a sip of tea, but barely even tasted it. "I should have known better."

"You should. As much as my son is a player, it is your fault you were taken in by him." Angelina did not hold back. "Players only pick those who they know they can play, and you chose to be played."

"I know, but I don't need you to lecture me."

"I've told you everything that you need to know about my son and now you're telling me not to lecture you. Would you rather I had lied for him?"

"No, but…" Leanne was not sure of what to say. "I'm sorry, but I don't like being judged."

"Everyone judges everyone. If we didn't we wouldn't know whom to trust and who not to. Everyone should be open to evaluation."

"Yeah, well, I don't like it," Leanne said sulkily. "People form their own opinion of me, but they don't know anything about me. That's why I hate it when people talk about me behind my back."

"There are two types of people: those who don't like to be talked about and those who do. The ones who don't like it know others are saying bad things about them, whereas the ones who do are aware that people are saying good things." Angelina did not mean to be cruel, but she also wanted to get her point across. "Which would you rather be?"

Again this made Leanne feel uncomfortable. Every time she tried to regain a bit of dignity she found herself being knocked back again. She was sure the woman opposite her was not deliberately being callous, but she still felt she was being somewhat harsh on her. "OK, so Bruno cheated on me and I probably should have seen it coming. I'm not perfect. I just wanted to meet someone. Is that so bad?" Leanne became agitated. "Don't forget that it was your son who did the cheating."

"I'm fully aware of that, and truly I'm embarrassed about it. I'm ashamed of the way he's behaved. I'm not saying it's entirely your fault, because it isn't. What I'm trying to tell you is that it's up to you to make sure it doesn't happen to you again, whether it's with my son or anyone else."

"I'm not going to let it happen again. I've been too nice for my own good and I'm going to change from now on. Good guys finish last."

Angelina had an exasperated look on her face. "Is that what you think? You really believe that good people come last in life and you're a good person?"

"Well, I'd like to think that good people get what they deserve, but that doesn't seem to be the case." Leanne brought her hand to her chest. "I believe that I'm a good person, and I certainly haven't come first with your son."

Angelina slowly shook her head. It was not a derogatory gesture, more an expression of pity. She genuinely felt sorry for the naive young woman sitting in front of her. It was not in her nature to let a dispute pass by without debate, so she continued.

"It's a fallacy. Good guys don't finish last. They finish first. But let's be clear about who we're talking about. For a start, it's not just 'guys'; it applies to girls as well." She tapped her finger on the table. "So to be clear, we're talking about everyone, no matter their gender or sexual orientation. But who is at the opposite end of the scale? If someone's not a good person, what are they?"

Leanne shrugged her shoulders. "A bad guy or girl, I suppose."

"Oh yes, the bastards and bitches," said Angelina with a sneer. "And there are enough of them in the world."

"I know. Your son's one of them." Leanne realised that she had overstepped the mark. "Sorry. I didn't mean to..."

"It's OK. I know what he's like. He's a clone of his father. Why do you think he's turned out like he has?" Angelina's expression became distant. "Bruno is like his dad. He has the same disregard for feelings, the same lack of respect for women and the same selfishness. I should know. I endured enough years suffering the same fate at the hands of his father."

"Really?"

"Yes, Bruno's dad treated me very badly. Before I divorced him, I spent over a decade being the victim and kept coming back for more. It was always my choice, though. He cheated on me, of course, but it was also the way he used me for his own means. I was like a fashion accessory to him. A certain sort of man likes to go out with an attractive woman on his arm. He likes to show her off. It gets so tiring trying to look your best all the time, to beat off the competition. He slowly stripped me of all my dignity, but only because I let him." Angelina lifted her chin in defiance. "I know better now, though. It took me a while, too long in fact, but I eventually worked out who finishes first with the bastards and bitches, and it's not the good guys and girls."

"What do you mean?"

"Well, for a start, who the hell wants to end up with a bastard or a bitch?"

"No one, I suppose."

"Exactly, but they do, don't they? People keep going back to them." Angelina gestured towards Leanne and then herself. "People like us. Women like a good-looking rogue, but why?"

"I've no idea." It was an honest response.

"There are a number of reasons. There's the excitement that a bad boy provides. You never know what he's going to do next. He will bring passion and excitement into the relationship, but the main reason we go for a rogue is stupidity." Angelina made no attempt to hide her own shortcomings. "We want to be the woman who changes the bad boy. It's all about our ego. We like to think that all the other women who tried to change him failed, but we will be the one who turns his life around. We actually believe that the other women aren't capable of winning him over, but we are. We're that naive we think other women are jealous of the man we've got by our side. But the worst thing we believe is that bad boys actually want to be good. They're bad because they want to be. They don't want to change."

Leanne was listening intently. Everything Angelina said rang true. Throughout the months she had been dating Bruno she knew what he was like, but wanted him to be something else. When they were walking down the street she wanted him to look at her lovingly, instead of leering at other women as they passed by. This applied to many aspects of their relationship. What she wanted was not what she was getting, but she had either convinced herself that she was satisfied or fooled herself into believing that things would change.

Angelina had not finished. "Men who go for bad girls are the same, but they're even more shallow than us when it comes to what others think. Some men would rather parade a bimbo in front of their friends, than a woman with principles. They're no different when they hope that a woman who's slept around is going to change for them." She sat back in her chair with a pensive look on her face. "You see, it's not the bitches and bastards we are attracted to who have got to change, it's us. And to do that you've got to realise one irrefutable truth; we are bad girls and bad boys too. Bitches and bastards attract bitches and bastards."

Leanne was not so sure about this last statement. "If someone treats me badly that doesn't make me a bitch," she protested.

"It does if the person who's treating you badly is yourself," she said. "You knew what Bruno was like the first moment you met him. All women can tell the difference between a bad boy and a gentleman. You started lying to yourself the moment you realised that you didn't like the truth. I know this, because it's what I used to do." A look of derision crossed her face, but it was aimed as much at herself as it was at the fragile young woman sitting opposite her.

"I've always treated those around me with respect. Not once have I ever deliberately mistreated a member of my family, a friend or even a stranger. Everyone who's ever known me has always thought that I am a good person, but I wasn't. I was an enemy to myself. If one of my friends had been with someone who was treating them badly I would have done my utmost to try and talk them out of that relationship, yet I would continuously subject myself to that same ill-treatment. What I would never have stood by and watched a loved one go through, I would deliberately inflict on myself. They say, 'treat others how you would like to be treated yourself', but when it came to me the saying should have been 'treat yourself how you treat others'. I was an angel to others, but a complete bitch to myself."

Angelina turned her head to the side and caught sight of her reflection in the oven door. She lowered her gaze, in a moment of self-reflection, almost as if she did not like what she saw. She was clearly a hard woman, but life had made her that way by breaking her heart. It may have healed, but the scars were still there. Seeing her son behave the same way as her ex-husband reminded her of the pain she had suffered and added to it. As much as this was as distressing she continued.

"When someone cheats in a relationship the first lie is told by the cheater, but the majority of lies told after that will be perpetrated by the one being cheated on." Angelina began to reel off a number of lines that she had fooled herself with. *"He was only talking to the stranger at the bar because she asked him what the time was. He turned his phone off when I walked into the room because he was buying my birthday present. He loves me.* I've heard them all, because I've said them all. I regularly and compulsively lied to myself."

"I've said a few of those things myself." Leanne shook her head in a defeated manner. "And I believed them as well."

"And that's why we're bitches. We lie to ourselves. There are those who treat their partners like dirt and those who are willing to be treated like dirt. Bitches and bastards want to be with bitches and bastards." Angelina's expression changed to one of contentment. "But on the other hand, a good girl knows the value of a good guy and vice versa. It takes a lady to appreciate a gentleman and a gentleman to appreciate a lady. It simply comes down to being who you want to be and then getting what you want. If you are a good girl you will get a good guy."

It all made sense. Leanne had been selling herself short with Bruno and every other man she had met before him. She had not been treating herself with respect and, as a result, the men in her life had treated her disrespectfully in return. There was no reason why she should carry on in this way. No man had the right to treat her badly and the only way they could get away with it was if she let them, and that had to change.

"So how do you go about getting what you want?" Leanne shrugged her shoulders. "I mean, is it that easy?"

"That's a good question. To get what you want you've first got to know what you want." Angelina got off her stool and walked over to a bookshelf on the far wall. "Have you actually thought about what you need from a relationship?"

"I don't really know."

"So you've never sat down and worked out what you want and, more importantly, what you don't want?"

"Maybe I haven't made that much of an effort."

"And that's the problem. When it comes to relationships people often don't know what they want." Angelina pulled a book from the shelf and came back again to sit down at the worktop. "I read this book a number of years ago. It's about why relationships flourish or fail. A psychologist by the name of Professor Madison Rose wrote it. She interviewed lots of people, couples, singles, etcetera, and got to know why their relationships were successful or broke down. It's called *The Farcical Rush*. It focuses on how people hurry into relationships without thinking about what they actually want out of them. That's why she calls it the farcical rush. People go head on into something that could affect them for the rest of their lives, but they don't consider the consequences. She identifies twelve factors that she calls the 'twelve labours of love' that are required to have a successful relationship. All twelve of them begin with each letter of the words 'Farcical Rush'."

Leanne was absorbing all that was being said to her. She had never thought about how she approached relationships before. It was always her intention to get with someone as quickly as possible to avoid being alone. There had not once been a set plan or any methodology to her actions. It was actually interesting to hear about the strategy in the book and she listened attentively as Angelina continued.

Angelina opened the book and flicked through the pages until she came to the one she wanted. "Ah, here it is. F is for favours; which means that you should be willing to put yourself out for your partner. A is autonomy; so you get to do what you want at times. R stands for resources; finances, necessary things like that. C is comeliness; which is looks. I is intercourse; you know what that is." Angelina gave a small smile after this one. "C is company; spending time together. A is attention; to show that you're being attentive your partner. L is loyalty; that's obvious. R is for respect; again obvious. U stands for understanding; knowing your partner. S is similarity; having things in common. And finally, H, honesty; being truthful to each other."

Angelina closed the book and put it down. "It's obvious really, isn't it? Yet few of us do it. People go into relationships without knowing what they do or don't want. You wouldn't go into a restaurant and ask for a beef pie if you're a vegan, would you? But people will get with someone who is moody, selfish, disloyal, and have all kinds of traits that aren't suitable for them. Of course, some people are desperate and they will eat whatever is put before them, but that's when it comes down to weighing up needs and self-respect. The question has to be asked whether being with someone is going to make you happier or not. It's not like buying the wrong newspaper and tomorrow you can get a different one. Relationships can last a lifetime." Angelina summed it all up plainly and simply. "It's about being aware of what you want for yourself and only accepting that."

Leanne sat nodding. This had certainly been a valuable lesson. Everything made sense to her. All she had to do was work out what she wanted, what she did not want, and then have enough respect for herself not to settle for anything less.

"Thanks, Angelina," she said. "I wasn't expecting this." Leanne smiled and looked embarrassed. "In fact, I thought you were going tell me that your son was too good for me."

"Darling, I would never be so predictable."

A lone figure sat at a window, gazing out across the town from a third-floor office block. He wore a grey roll necked jumper and beige corded trousers. His spectacles were balanced on the end of his nose and his lacklustre hair was combed over his forehead. With moccasins on his feet and a few days of stubble on his chin his appearance was extremely casual, as you would expect from a counsellor.

In his late thirties, Gavin had fashioned a successful career after graduating from university. He could have chosen most types of occupational psychology to have gone into, but the demands of working in the sex abuse sector appealed to him most, and it was also easier to get into than other areas of counselling due to the unpopular nature of the work. A person needed to be very resilient to listen to some of the accounts that their clients would sometimes divulge, and when it came to mental strength, he had loads of it.

Gavin was wheelchair bound. He had developed muscular dystrophy at a young age and it had severely affected the muscles in his legs. When he was at school he had managed to struggle around using leg braces, but now he had no choice but to remain permanently seated throughout the day. However, his physical disability had been no barrier to a successful career.

What Gavin had lost in physical strength in his legs, he more than made up for with mental resolve. The weight that he carried with his job proved that. Not many people could sit and listen to a paedophile talk about their crimes and not crumble under the load. When it came to carrying such a cumbersome burden, Gavin was more than capable, and this was just as well as his fortitude was about to be tested once more.

Oliver was sitting at a desk in the centre of the office filling out forms. He had spent the last ten minutes reading them and signing each one in turn. It was compulsory for him to agree to the set conditions as part of his sentence, and any refusal of the terms would mean a direct visit to prison. When he had, finally, completed all of the paperwork he put down the pen and sat back in his chair without saying a word.

Gavin had continued looking out of the window, but when he noticed the cessation of the sound of paper being turned he turned around and realised that his attention was now required. He wheeled himself over to the desk and had a quick glance at each of the forms to make sure they had been filled in correctly. When he was satisfied that everything was in order he explained the process of the counselling sessions he would be providing in the coming months.

"OK, let's start. Those papers you've signed state the rules you have to abide by. After a period of time some of them may become relaxed, whereas others may stay in place indefinitely, depending on your progress. So, to clarify what you can't do: no contact with children or minors without informing me or my office, no possession of a phone or tablet with a camera, no alcohol or drugs, no unapproved relationships, and no use of the internet to view anything that is in any way related to your crimes." Gavin glanced at Oliver over the top of his glasses. "Do you understand?"

"Yes."

"Good. Now I'm going to explain how we're going to approach your counselling sessions from moving forward. First of all, today, we are going to talk about your past and try to identify why you have become who and what you are. In later weeks we will discuss such things as how you are going to take responsibility for your actions, scenarios that might trigger you to reoffend, empathy for your victims, the pursuit of a healthy sex life, and behavioural techniques to help you manage your deviant sexual fantasies. Keep in mind that these are just some of the subjects we will approach." Gavin paused to allow Oliver time to absorb this information. "Is there anything that you don't understand so far?"

"No."

"Right, so let's get to the five W's. Who, what, when, where and why?"

Gavin sat back and looked at Oliver expectantly. A reply was not, however, forthcoming; just an apathetic stare and a sullen silence. This would not do at all.

Gavin was not about to let the first session start off at such a slow pace and he went about making his intentions clear. Although he would not accept having his work undermined, he was aware that he could not force the person before him to divulge something that they did not want to. The manner in which he prompted an acceptable response was both professional and sympathetic.

"I know what you went through. It was in your pre-sentence report. You told the probation officer that you were abused when you were young. That's why you're not in prison right now." Gavin took off his glasses, folded them and then put them on the desk in front of him so that his eyes were clearly visible. "The court recognised that you were a victim before you became an offender. You're being given the chance to change. This is your opportunity to put things right, and keep your actions in the past so that they don't affect your future."

This was not what Oliver was expecting. He was expecting to be told that he was worthless, sick in the head and beyond redemption. It never occurred to him that he could actually have a chance to live a normal life. That was not something he had been allowed to do since he was an infant. His father saw to that. He wondered if it might be worth setting free what was locked away in his mind.

Oliver shuffled uneasily in his seat. It would not be easy for him to talk about the past. He had never done it before and there was a good reason for that. The humiliation of describing how he was sexually abused was a horrific thought to him. However, there was a part of him that wanted to get it all out into the open and shedding that load certainly felt appealing. When he finally spoke it was in a quiet and cautious voice.

"What do you want to know?"

"Why don't we start with who hurt you?" Gavin's words were chosen carefully. "Take your time and say only as much as you want to."

"It was my father. There was nothing I could do to stop it." Oliver's mouth felt dry, making it difficult to speak, but he carried on regardless. "He had this way of just…"

It was at this point that the past met the present, the truth came out and facts were laid bare. Everything that had happened to Oliver was described in full. The garden shed, the dark bedroom and the evenings when his mother went to bed early were all relayed. Once he began talking, he found he could not stop and not one revolting detail or harrowing emotion was left out. Everything was unleashed for the first time. Oliver journeyed through hell once more and his ordeal lasted for over forty-five minutes.

Oliver felt physically sick. To bring it all up was to live it again. It was like there had been a knife embedded in his side that had fallen out years ago, leaving a deep wound, but had now been put back in again in exactly the same place. Feelings of humiliation, defilement and helplessness once again laid siege to his mind. However, on this occasion, there was one difference. When he was young all the sickening turmoil had been forced on him. This time he was in control, not his father.

Gavin had heard enough for now. It had been hard to listen to such a disturbing account of child abuse. Nevertheless, it was his job and he went about bringing clarity to it all.

"So that's the five W's. Who, what, when, where and why. 'Who' was your father. 'What' was what he did to you. 'When' was as a child. 'Where' was where no one else could witness it. 'Why' was because he was sick." The next words were spoken without emotion, but were well-chosen. "And this is why you are like you are now."

Oliver nodded slowly and closed his eyes. It was true. He had become his father and it felt awful to realise it. There was no one he loathed more and yet he had turned into a replica of him. This was both heart-breaking and horrifying.

Although he realised that he had hit a nerve, Gavin carried on with his assessment. "There was nothing you could have done at the time, but your actions since then are your fault. The path you have taken was of your own choosing, but there are other ways a person can turn out after they have been abused as a child. It comes down to how they deal with the fact that what happened to them was out of their control.

"Some people who have suffered a similar trauma try to trivialise it. For instance, they might become prostitutes or go into the porn industry. They do this for two reasons. One is because they think that by letting someone abuse them in adult life they can make the unacceptable acceptable. They then feel what they endured as a child wasn't that bad. The other reason is because when it happened to them when they were a child they, were not in control, but by letting someone abuse them they get back a sense of self-will. Of course, neither of these options can be considered desirable. Letting yourself be defiled is not a lot different to having it forced on you. You're still being treated less than humanely whether you allow it or not. You, however, have gone the other way. In order to get back the control that you didn't have when you were a child, you seek control over others. That is why you have these extremely harmful compulsions which are as much about empowerment as they are sexual desire. This is not at all acceptable and it has to change. To do this you need to accept your past, get it under control in the present and make sure you never succumb to such thoughts in the future."

"How can I do that?" Oliver's voice was awash with hopelessness. "I wish I could change what has happened, but I can't."

"You can't change the past, but you can decide on your own future. To do that you must, first of all, set yourself free from your father." Gavin explained it as simply as possible. "When you were a child you had no choice about whether you were a victim, but now you must choose not to be. You see, crime is society's punishment for when children have a bad upbringing. Most criminal offenders are victims before they make society their victim. A temperamental father can create a thug who beats people up, and a drunken mother can produce a drug addict who steals to feed their habit. Thieves, murderers and all sorts of criminals are most likely forged by bad parents, whereas good parents are more inclined to create doctors, teachers and the more accomplished members of society. Of course, good parents can create bad people, and bad parents can create good people, but as far as you are concerned that is not the case. Your father created a paedophile. You must undo that. You weren't born like your father, but when you became an adult you chose to be like him. So now you can change again. It's up to you. Do not become the person who hurt you. You have to stop the flow of blood to the wound that has been inflicted on you, so that you don't inflict the same wound on someone else."

"This is not just about me is it?" said Oliver, who was starting to reflect on everything that had happened and was becoming more aware of his own dire faults. "Those photos I took had victims in them as well. If those children knew what I had done they would hate me as much as I despise my father. Of all people, I should know how it feels to be a victim. This has got to stop. I need to make sure that this sickness ends with me, so it doesn't spread to anyone else. It can't go on."

"That's right. You must never again create another victim. You can't risk creating another 'you'. The battle you must fight from here onwards is between the present you and the old you, so you can create the new you. You can't change yourself unless you admit that who you are now is not acceptable. If you don't look back at what you have done and admit that it was terrible you will not want to reform your ways. You must first hate yourself in the past in order to love yourself in the future. This is not going to be easy, but the rewards of having a normal life will be worth it."

"I will do whatever it takes." Oliver's expression was resolute and he sat up in his chair. "I have to."

Gavin could see that his client had grasped the essence of what he had said. This would not be enough, though. He knew that the threat of prison was not enough to make someone like this change, they had to be encouraged to go in the right direction. It was with this in mind that he explained the path he was outlining.

"Ask yourself this; who achieves more? Someone who is brought up by good parents, who is taught right and wrong, and who is loved from an early age? Or a person who battles to overcome anguish and pain, who has evil bred into them, who has to learn right and wrong on their own, and who has never been taught what love is? Some people are born halfway up the mountain and some start right at the top, but others have to climb up from the bottom. Life is not easy when you start at the lowest point, but when you reach the summit it feels a lot better than it does for those who began there. In fact, halfway up can feel like the top of the world." Gavin summed it up in one sentence. "This must be your purpose in life."

Oliver did not reply. No response was necessary. He knew what he had to do and so did the person opposite him. With a determined expression he simply nodded once and that was all.

There were about a dozen people of all ages sitting in a circle, facing one another. None of them looked like they wanted to be there. Most of them wore glum expressions, and the few who were smiling seemed to be insincere.

This was the last place Emma wanted to be; a drugs counselling session for lost souls that society had misplaced. Since losing her job she had accepted that something needed to be done about her drug habit, whereas previously she had always denied having a problem. As for her mental health issues, she had barely even acknowledged their existence, let alone discussed them with anyone. To actually reveal her weaknesses to other people would make her feel vulnerable and the thought of that was not pleasant.

All the people in the circle wore a sticky label with their names written on it, in thick pen, apart from one. The only person who had a plastic badge was the drugs counsellor who was leading the session. He was there every week, whereas some of the others were, unfortunately, less consistent with their attendance.

Ryan was a middle-aged man with gaunt features and a skinny frame. His complexion was rough and his eyes had heavy bags underneath them. With his unshaven chin and unkempt clothes it looked like he was the last person who should be giving out valuable life advice. Appearances can be deceiving though.

If someone is going to be told not to do drugs it is better that it comes from someone who speaks from experience. Only a person who has suffered the despair of dependence can truly explain the pain of addiction. Every word they say is genuine and every emotion they express is from the heart. The members of the group were about to observe this first-hand.

"OK, we're all here." Ryan started the session. "I want to begin by welcoming a new member to the group. Everyone, this is Emma." He motioned towards her with his hand.

All the heads turned to look at the latest attendee. This was rather embarrassing, but to be expected. Every person there had been through this uncomfortable experience at some point. There were a few nods and half smiles in her direction, and Emma responded by forcing a grin which disappeared as quickly as it had materialised.

Ryan waited for a moment to let the obligatory polite, but unenthusiastic, greetings pass and then continued. "At the end of last week's session I was asked by one of the group to describe how I see cocaine. This was a really good question which I couldn't answer at the time, so I gave myself a few days to think of my response." He paused to gather his thoughts. "So I'm going to start by giving my description of the demon that ruined my life for so many years."

Ryan waited a moment before continuing to make sure he had everyone's attention. This was not easy for him. Although he had spoken about his drug addiction in public many times before, it was still an uncomfortable thing to do. No one likes to be self-critical, even though it is essential in order to self-heal. He spoke in a soft voice.

"She's absolutely beautiful. If you could describe cocaine as a living being she would be a stunning woman that lights up the room, or a man so handsome he blows you away with his smile. For me, she's utterly stunning and captivates you whenever she's around." Ryan sat with his head bowed, but his voice was loud enough for everyone to hear. "When you first meet her she steals your heart within minutes. For days after she's all you think about. You can't wait until the next time you're together, and when it comes she doesn't disappoint. She is exceptional at what she does."

Everyone in the room sat with their gaze steadfastly fixed on Ryan. They could all relate exactly to what he was talking about. The way he was speaking so positively about his nemesis was a true reflection of how they felt about theirs too. Although they all hated drugs, they loved them too. His words were spoken with a passion that they all knew only too well.

"Every time you go out you want her there. You feel on top of the world when you're with her. It's like everyone else can see how happy you are together and you want to share your happiness with them too. The more time you spend together the more you fall in love. You even start having her back at yours during weekdays. It doesn't matter if you've got work the next day and you don't mind how late you stay up. All you care about is spending time with her. She's the only thing you think about. She's fantastic. She's awesome. She's absolutely beautiful." His face suddenly changed to one of disgust. "But she's also a cruel, heartless bitch!"

Ryan sat back in his chair and looked around the circle as he gave his damning verdict. "She ruins every aspect of your life. You can't get her out of your mind. If she doesn't call you every night, she definitely calls you each weekend. It's not like you can delete her number. There's not a moment when she's not whispering into your ear. There's never a let up. Everything you do centres around her. All the things you used to enjoy doing you don't bother with anymore. She is all that matters. Your money will go before you know it. Bills go unpaid and you make sure you've got cash for her before anything else. You borrow money from those closest to you, even though you know you can't pay them back, so you avoid the people you care about because she forces you to choose her over them. You think that no one knows you're spending so much time with her, but everyone sees it. She turns you against your family and friends. They tell you she's bad for you, but you ignore them. They hate her, but you take her side every time. This is when the lying starts, but not just about her, about everything. There's a different story for every time you screw up. Whether you turn up late, miss an appointment or let someone down, it's always accompanied by feeble excuses that no one falls for. The fact that you think everyone believes you is the most ignorant act of all. Worst of all, though, most of the lies you tell are to yourself. I'm fine, it doesn't matter, and I'll sort it out tomorrow; you actually believe your own crap. By the time she's got her talons deep into your flesh it's too late. She is inside your body, mind and soul, and she's not leaving. You are in a battle now, and it's one you don't mind if you lose, so what chance have you got of winning? You start to hate her, but you still can't tear yourself away. With no work, no money and no respect from those who care about you, you're at rock bottom. She's all you've got left. It's just you and her. Your life has been ruined by this merciless, cruel bitch. But even after everything that has gone on, with all of the devastation, the tears and heartache, after all the lies and denials, there's only one thing that you are one hundred per cent sure of." He closed his eyes to shut out the anguish. "She's absolutely beautiful."

This was met with silence as those present reflected on what they had just heard. It was hard for some of them to listen to their nemesis being described in a positive light considering the hardship it had brought to their life. They only had negative thoughts about this heinous demon. Even though it unsettled them to hear such a paradoxical portrayal they all knew it was an accurate and honest description of their affliction.

"So, how do people go from not doing drugs at all to becoming an addict?" Ryan continued. "It doesn't always happen overnight. Cocaine is an enemy that can slowly sneak up on you. With me, it happened quite quickly. The first few times I took it I was in control, but with drugs the more you do them the more they take control of you. The people who are most likely to become addicts are the ones who say they won't become an addict. This is because they don't think they have to fight against it, so keep doing it as much as they like. There's not a person on this planet who can take drugs four or five times a week and not find themselves developing a habit. I thought I was invincible. I was wrong. But how do you go from being in a position where everything in your life is fine to the point that you find yourself in trouble? Well, in the years I've been counselling I've determined that there are five degrees of exposure. They are abstinence, casual, recreational, habitual and addict. This applies not only to drugs, but also to gambling, drinking and other activities that can lead to over-attachment. So I'll explain each one in detail. Abstinence is obviously someone who never drinks, smokes or takes drugs. They don't even try it. I'm sure we all wish we were in that category." Ryan looked around at the group and smiled. "Casual is when someone gambles on a big horserace that happens once a year or maybe does a line of coke at a wedding because other people are doing it. They do it as a one off. Recreational is when someone does it as a means of enjoyment, as regularly as going clubbing, out for friends' birthdays or when their wages are paid at the end of the month. Habitual is when someone exposes themselves every time they are in a social situation, spend time with like-minded people or they can't even walk past the bookmakers without going in to check the odds. They set aside money for drugs, drinking or gambling to the point that their habits get paid for even before the bills and other essentials. Addiction is when someone is completely dependent on their stimulant. They have to gamble every day or have a bottle of vodka for breakfast. They are addicted to the point that they simply can't function unless they have had their fix. I couldn't even go to work without doing a line of cocaine. The important thing to recognise is that every individual is different when it comes to the distance between each of the five degrees of exposure. They can be close or far apart depending on the person. Some people might place one bet or experience one hit of a drug and then rapidly slide towards habit or addiction, whereas for others it might take longer depending on their level of contact with their fix. However, no matter who the individual is, the more they expose themselves, the greater the certainty that they will develop an addiction. It is also as well to know that the gaps between each of the degrees of exposure are not the same in distance. The gap between abstinence and being a casual user is a big one, but the distances get smaller and smaller the further along the scale you go. If someone develops a habit, the possibility of it quickly turning into an addiction is extremely high. There's not a lot separating the two. Needless to say, the best thing is to avoid doing any of it, but life is never that simple. But we all know that."

Sometimes in his counselling sessions Ryan would give the attendees time to ponder over what they had heard, whether it was him who had said it or someone else in the group. Silence was an excellent tool for getting people to think for themselves. It was one he used often and to good effect. However, on this occasion, he felt it was a good time to move the session on so picked someone to continue the momentum.

"Emma, could you tell us why you're here please?"

This was an unexpected and unwelcome request. To be put under the spotlight like was uncomfortable, embarrassing and belittling. The response was aloof and awkward.

"I'd rather not." Emma lowered her gaze. "I don't think I'm ready for that."

"It's OK. We all know it's not easy." Ryan was not about to force her into anything, but was also unwilling to give up so easily. "You can start by telling us a little about yourself. It's easier than you think."

Although this was an unpleasant situation to be in, Emma felt it would not be too bad to say a little bit about herself. She did not plan to disclose too much, just enough to satisfy the group and make her seem a part of the proceedings. She might be attending the group, but did not feel as though she wanted to be a part of it.

"My mind has always worked differently. I've never been comfortable with my own thoughts. That's why I take drugs."

Ryan was experienced in his field of counselling and knew how to deal with Emma's reluctance to speak about her problems. He was aware that there was a lot more to this young woman than she was willing to divulge and he knew exactly how to get it into the open. Not by coaxing it out of her, but by using one of the other group members.

"Anna, why don't you tell everyone the reason you got into drugs?" The choice of this particular individual was no accident. "You can be brief or elaborate. It's up to you, and you can tell us in your own time."

Ryan pretty much knew everything about Anna. She had been coming to his drugs rehabilitation sessions for almost two years. She had been clean for the same amount of time. Although she was still an addict, and always would be, she was a non-user who accepted she had an addiction. It was why she had got into using narcotics that he wanted her to talk about, and she did not disappoint.

"I've got mental health problems. That's why I started using. For me it was always about repressing what I couldn't understand or control. It was the wrong way of going about it, but I didn't know any better." Anna got straight to the point and did not mind being ruthless in her self-appraisal. "From an early age I knew I was nothing like the other kids at school. I had anger issues and I regularly got into fights. The violence I suffered at the hands of my mother was redistributed to other children in the classroom. Post Traumatic Stress Disorder (PTSD), they call it. An ashtray to the shins or a cigarette on the back of the hand tends to destabilise a child. I became a horrible bitch, and because I got away with it there was no reason to stop. All the victims I created meant nothing to me, because I didn't realise that I was transferring my pain on to them. That's why my anguish was still there, unrecognised and untreated. And that's where drugs came in; the ultimate painkillers and pain-makers."

Anna was relaxed and calm. She spoke like she was talking about buying groceries from her local supermarket. It was amazing how she could talk so casually about a subject that was clearly so traumatic, and showed on the faces of the others present. Not one person wore anything other than an expression of respect and awe.

Although Anna was a short woman, she had a sturdy frame. It looked like she was capable of carrying two-dozen bricks up three sets of ladders. Her lined and weathered face appeared as though she had lived a life of hard labour. She did not seem like the sort of person to hold back in any situation, and she was certainly not about to let up in her current one.

"Cocaine led to heroin. No surprise there. When you think you're unbeatable you're willing to take on any opponent. Unfortunately for me, I didn't realise that my battle was with myself. It was only when my body and mind were smashed to pieces that I realised I had beaten up my final victim; me." Anna spoke with pride. "But that's when I made a change. I got up. I got to my feet and I took the first step; the hardest step. I took a look at myself. As much as I didn't like what I saw, I showed my reflection to everyone. I joined this group and, for the first time in my life, I spoke about my past to complete strangers. After that, it was a lot easier to talk about it to those closest to me, my family and what few friends I had managed to keep. At last I could open up about my mental health problems, my drug addiction and everything else I had kept bottled up inside. And that was how it started. The thing I was once embarrassed about, and ashamed of, I slowly began to talk about openly and without hesitation. So now I'm not even slightly flustered when discussing it, because why would you feel humiliated about your greatest victory? Yeah, it's an ongoing battle, and always will be, but I'm winning it and I'm clean. I'm a drug addict, who suffers from PTSD, and that won't change, but I'm no loser. I'm on top of the world."

The room was silent; no one said a word. A round of applause would have seemed condescending and insulting. There did not need to be a declaration of the victor on this occasion as it was so obvious. It was plain to see who the winner was.

Emma in awe. She could not believe that someone could be so brutal and yet so soul-searching in their self-appraisal. This was not something she had even tried in her own life, let alone done so honestly and thoroughly. Before her this woman had just ruthlessly criticised herself in front of everyone, and yet had shown nothing but an unwavering strength and resolve in doing so. It was incredible.

Up until this point, Emma had thought there was no one who would comprehend the contents of her mind, but now it seemed there were others who might have similar stories to tell. Maybe they were not suffering from the same ailments, but the symptoms of anguish and hurt were certainly comparable. In the past, Emma had always felt alone in her suffering, but it appeared there were others who might understand her, and that felt great.

For the first time in her life, Emma felt as if not only could she be capable of talking about herself and her past, but she actually wanted to. Not only did she feel a desire to reveal all, but a need to. It would be like stripping herself of the chains that had been wrapped around her for years.

"I see things that aren't there," said Emma, glancing at Ryan. He nodded for her to continue. "I have done since I was young. It's spiders normally, but it can be other things. It can happen at any time, but usually if I'm under some kind of stress. It makes a bad situation worse." Emma had wind in sails now and she let it blow her full speed ahead. "I also have a compulsive urge to count numbers, match shapes and repeat patterns. It takes full control of me sometimes. I don't know why I have to do it, but I just do. Not being in control of my own mind is awful. I mean, it's my brain and yet there are times when I don't have a say over how it thinks or what it sees. Even my feelings don't belong to me at times. That's probably the worst part."

Emma turned her hands so that her palms were facing upwards. This revealed a number of scars on her wrists, just visible in between the multiple bangles she was wearing. She slowly shook her head, but carried on with her very public introspection.

"I've also self-harmed. Drugs stopped all of that for a while. Cocaine offered me a way out, if only for a short time. Even a short break from the mental pain was a welcome respite, but that's the problem. It didn't last. Nothing changed. It didn't do anything to heal what was already in my mind and instead created more problems, most of which were even worse. I'm not a nice person anymore. I've lost my friends, I've got no job, my life is a mess, and what part of my mind that was functioning properly is now controlled by my dependence on drugs." Emma breathed out an exasperated sigh and then looked around. "I can't go on like this. I've got to sort myself out in every aspect of my life. I need to change."

It was a moment of clarity. For Emma to actually acknowledge to herself that she had an issue with her mental health was like being freed from a prison cell. Now that she knew she had a problem she could address it and deal with it. Being aware of the imperfections of her mind and accepting that she needed help was the first step of a journey that would take her to a place where she wanted to exist. With the help of others, she would be able to talk about it without being embarrassed or find solutions of how to deal with it and that, in turn, would help with her drug problem.

Emma had a bad cocaine habit, and now that she had admitted that to herself she could do something about it. It wouldn't be easy, life isn't, but it can certainly be easier if you're going in the right direction. She had taken the first step of acknowledging that she had a drug problem and could make a start on the road to rehabilitation. Her feelings of relief were echoed by those around her.

"It feels good, doesn't it?"

"I remember my first time talking about it. It was great."

"No better feeling that showing your feelings."

It appeared as though everyone there had, at some point, taken the first step that Emma had just done. They all knew what it was like to pull up the anchor and set sail on their own voyage of self-discovery and healing. It would be a long and sometimes strenuous crossing through some very stormy seas, but the final destination would be well worth it. Maybe she would not find a chest full of gold at the end of it, but at least there would not be the eternal pain and suffering. That alone would make the journey worthwhile.

From that point on the counselling session carried on in the same vein. One after the other the attendees spoke of their own addictions, problems and past. Some described their stories more candidly than others, and some shed a tear at the damage they had done those closest to them as well as themselves. Not one person judged anyone. They all listened and showed support no matter what anyone said or how low they had fallen.

Lisa told the group how she felt about having an abortion in her teens and how she had subsequently turned to drugs to numb the guilt. Jim spoke about how his father had kept leaving the family home and coming back when he was a child, so his insecurities had led to depression, which was then treated with cocaine. These were just some of the stories that were told, but each of them was followed by heart-warming tales of working towards recovery and redemption. This was a group of people going forward by using the present to reflect on the past, and it worked.

As Emma sat there pondering her newfound mental freedom she felt a wave of relief rush over her. For once, she was not alone in her suffering and she could battle her demons with the help of others. She would be able to discuss her mental health with those who understood her torment and could seek advice about her compulsion for drugs from people who cared. This was exactly what she needed, even though just hours ago she had no idea what she even wanted. Salvation was in sight and, at last, it looked like it was attainable.

Chapter 7

Leanne, Oliver, Vincent and Emma's lives had all taken a turn for the better. They had unexpectedly seen a glimpse of who they were and they did not like it. Once they had looked back at their home lives and realised why they had become who they were, they made the courageous decision to change. It had not been easy for any of them to look in the mirror and see such an unfavourable reflection, but it had been necessary and, as a result, they were willing to transform their lives. The road to a better future would be long, but it was a journey worth embarking upon. Every decision they made from now on would have to be the right one, but that is easier said than done.

Life can be unpredictable and cruel. Sometimes events take place which leave a person in a position where the choices that are available to them can make or break them. It is at times like these when a person has to choose a path that will either be the right one or the wrong one, and their decision could affect them for the rest of their days. Such turning points must always be approached with a prepared mind, because they will most certainly come around. In fact, it would be just a matter of time before all four young adults would be tested.

As Leanne wandered around the supermarket she barely read the labels on any of the products as she put them in her basket. It was not that she did not care about what she was buying; she couldn't be bothered to think about such frivolous details. There were other things on her mind that were far more pressing.

On Friday she was going to go to a party at a work colleague's house and she was wondering what to wear. The new blue dress that had been delivered during the week was nice, but she was rather fond of the white one she had bought in the spring. As for what shoes to wear, that would depend on what handbag she would take with her. Such decisions were important and required careful consideration.

The party was going to be a quiet affair with not too many people there. Mostly couples, a handful of single women and one or two unattached men were to be expected, and that was how Leanne wanted it. She was not in the mood for a relationship right now. Being on her own made a pleasant change and it had freed up her time to do other things, such as joining a gym and catching up on several series on Netflix she had been meaning to watch for some time. Everything was OK; maybe not great, but good enough.

Leanne's plan to change her life was to abstain from men, at least in the short term. She had no intention of being single forever, just long enough to get her head straight. The best way to go about that was to remove temptation from her life. No clubbing, no bars and a mass deletion of contact numbers from her mobile were measures that had been implemented. So far it seemed to be working.

No one can be tempted if what they are obsessed with is out of reach. A compulsive gambler can't lose their money if there is no means of betting, just as a drug addict cannot feed their habit if there are no narcotics at hand. The problem is that often temptation comes to the afflicted.

"Hi," said a familiar voice from behind Leanne. "I haven't seen you in a while."

She did not need to turn around to know who it was, but did so anyway and looked into those piercing eyes once more. A conversation could not possibly lead to anything anyway. Besides, it is rude not to reply when someone is talking to you.

Bruno stood there self-assuredly, wearing his well-practised smile. Conceit oozed out of every pore. When he spoke, his words were like liquid silver as they slipped off his tongue.

"You look great. I've really missed you. In fact, I was thinking about you only this morning as I passed the lake we used to sit by in the park."

Leanne began to walk away, but it was just a token gesture. Bruno was quick to react. Like a fish caught on an angler's hook, he reeled her back in. His words changed direction, but they led to the same destination.

"Look, I don't blame you for being mad at me. I was out of order. I shouldn't have accepted a lift home from her. That kiss was a bad choice; a mistake." It was like he was reading the script from a poorly written play. "I realise that I hurt you and that's the worst thing about it. I feel awful. Ever since it happened I've wanted to apologise. I'm sorry. I really, really am."

As the front door closed it sent an echo through the large entrance hall. The surroundings were both familiar and welcoming. There was no awkwardness in the atmosphere and it felt good. They had both been there before as a couple and here they were again; a rekindling of the past.

Bruno took Leanne's coat and she sent a smile his way to show her appreciation of the gesture. The whole act was playing out like clockwork. It seemed nothing could halt the inevitable move to the bedroom, until someone else entered the room.

Angelina strolled into the hall and began putting on a long coat. The moment she saw her son and his partner she stopped in her tracks. Normally, she would have greeted them both, but on this occasion she said nothing.

Bruno was unaware of any awkwardness. "Hi, Mum," he said. "Where are you going?"

Angelina did not reply. She finished adjusting her coat and put the strap of her bag over her shoulder. It was obvious that she did not want to stay around to exchange any pleasantries. As she made her way to the door she deliberately avoided eye contact with Leanne.

Just then, Bruno's phone started ringing and he immediately pulled it out of his pocket. After a quick glance at the screen, he said, "Oh, that's work. They probably need to talk to me about the project I'm working on. I'll only be a few minutes." At that, he hurriedly made his way into the kitchen and closed the door.

Leanne had turned away as soon as she saw Angelina. She did not want to see the expression on her face. She felt embarrassed that she was being so weak. The situation was extremely uncomfortable and the sooner it ended the better.

Angelina had reached the front door, but had chosen not to open it. Instead, she stood there with her head bowed. Although she had somewhere else to be, she felt she had to say something to Leanne.

"I spent years doing what you are doing right now and there's not a day that goes by that I don't regret it. I wish I could go back in time so that I could make the right decisions." Angelina slowly shook her head. "It may seem like a strange thing to say, but I wish I was in your position right now, because I would love to walk away and put things right. I envy you."

"It's not what you think. We're just going to talk."

"Oh really!" Angelina turned towards her with a sad expression. "If you want to lie to yourself, darling, that's up to you, but I've told myself enough lies over the years, I don't need to hear anymore."

Leanne closed her eyes to shut out the awkwardness of the situation. She did not want to be there. All she wanted was to get on with her life and be free to make her own decisions. She would worry about the consequences later.

Angelina spoke in a quiet and subdued voice. "Do you know what finally made me change my life?"

"No."

"*De Profundis.*"

"I'm sorry, what?" Leanne did not understand.

"Have you heard of Oscar Wilde?"

"Wasn't he a writer?"

"Yes, but he was also a poet and a playwright. And he was brilliant. His best piece of work, though, was written when he was in prison, and it wasn't even a book, poem or a play. It was a letter to his lover. It got published years later and was given the title *De Profundis*. It's Latin for 'from the depths'. A close friend of mine suggested that I read it when I was at my lowest, so I did. And thank God I did, because it changed my life."

"Was it a love letter?" This was an optimistically hollow question in the hope that what Leanne was about to hear was a romantic story.

"Oh, it was much more than that, darling. He wrote it to his former lover, Lord Alfred Douglas, but he addressed him by his nickname, 'Bosie'. You see, Oscar Wilde was gay. That's why he was in prison. In the late nineteenth century it was against the law for two men to have a relationship. The crime of 'gross indecency' too often carried a prison sentence.

"At the beginning of the letter Oscar recounts their extravagant lifestyle, ill-fated relationship and how it affected his work. Bosie didn't have a lot of money, but regularly made demands that they eat at posh restaurants and stay at expensive hotels, which Oscar frequently succumbed to and paid for himself. When Bosie was ill, Oscar cared for him, but when Oscar was ill, Bosie left him to suffer alone. While they spent time together, Oscar stated that his writing had become sterile, but when they were apart it flourished. Bosie had had a negative effect on Oscar's life and work, and the letter made that clear." Angelina stepped forward to catch Leanne's eye, to make sure she was taking it all on board.

"It is important to understand the true reason Oscar wrote the letter; not to blame Bosie for everything that had gone wrong, but to blame himself. Oscar had chosen to do all the things that had destroyed his life. He gave in to all of Bosie's wishes, he pretended there was compassion when there was little, and he let this person break his heart. Oscar Wilde made every decision that led to his downfall. He built his own prison cell. Just like us. You and I have done exactly the same thing. We've let someone else dictate how our lives will go. We did so out of foolish pride and unrestrained ego. I know you won't read *De Profundis*, Leanne, you don't need to. Take it from someone who has. You must not ruin your life for someone else. If you do, you only have yourself to blame."

Angelina opened the front door, ready to leave. As she did so she paused and turned to Leanne.

"It's up to you now, darling," she said in a calm voice. She glanced towards the staircase. "Either you go up those stairs or leave this house now. This is one of the most significant turning points in your life."

Angelina left and the door closed behind her, leaving only silence. Leanne found herself with those final words going around in her head. It all came down to this moment. The choice was hers; a decision that would define her future.

At that moment, Bruno reappeared and stood in the entrance hall looking at Leanne expectantly.

It had been a stressful week. A lot more packages had been delivered to the warehouse than normal and there was a backlog of stock that needed to be stored. It had taken a great deal of hard work, but the job had finally been completed. For this effort a stiff drink was needed to help him relax and as a reward.

Vincent was sitting at the bar on one of the high stools. He had only just walked in and had not even ordered yet, but a bottle of beer was placed in front of him regardless. He smiled at the person who had put it there.

Barbara raised an eyebrow as she spoke. "Been hard at work?"

"Yeah! Forty per cent increase of incoming stock." Vincent breathed out an exhausted sigh. "There's even more due next week."

"Still, it's a job. You can't complain about that these days, with so many people out of work."

"Yup, I've actually got money in the bank for once." This was followed by a proud smile.

"Does that mean I might get a tip?" Barbara said with a wily grin.

"Well, I'd give you money for a drink, but I'm not rich and water is free."

It was a meaningful joke, but they both laughed. The two of them knew alcohol had played a big part in their problems, but only one completely abstained from it. Some people can't handle even one glass of liquor, whereas others have a higher limit. It's down to each individual to know their cut off point. There are some who know where this is and others who have never bothered to find out. Such people, who drink beyond that boundary, tend not to care about the people it affects.

Although Barbara and Vincent had had their problems in life they were very different people, nonetheless. She had made many mistakes throughout her life and had paid for them dearly, whereas he had made just a few and had got away with the majority of them. This was why Barbara had chosen complete abstinence from alcohol, and Vincent had set himself a limit of about six or seven bottles. Both of their approaches seemed to work and they had not done anything detrimental towards themselves, or others, for some time. All they had to do was keep up their guard.

As the night wore on the drink flowed. The atmosphere in the bar was one of cheerfulness and respite. Vincent had got into a conversation with two young women who appeared to be comfortable in his company. They seemed to like his jokes and he was fond of their attention. He had even bought them drinks and they had done likewise, to the point that he had drunk slightly more than he would normally allow himself to. One or two over the limit surely wouldn't hurt and he doubted that anything could ruin his evening.

Two groups of men, in the pub, had been drinking heavily all evening and had resorted to exchanging banter between each other. It started as harmless fun and both sides had laughed at the jokes aimed at them. Unfortunately, one of the men had drunk a great deal too much and inadvertently made a remark that had gone too far. He apologised straight away when he realised that he had overstepped the mark, but one of the men in the other group was not willing to let it lie.

Alcohol changes people, but only to a certain degree. It does not change their personality, but instead alters their perception of what is right or wrong. Someone might imagine that they could take on a professional boxer, from the comfort of their living room, but when they come face to face with such an individual their sense of reality kicks in and they accept that they are not capable of doing so. However, when they are drunk they might lose their inhibitions and believe they are capable of fighting four men on their own. This applies to morals and principles as well. They might say something they would never normally say or be offended by something that would not usually bother them. That is the mist that blinds people when they are intoxicated.

A few men from each group were trying to calm the situation down. Others preferred not to get involved. The man who had taken offence was behaving very aggressively and raising his voice. As for the man who had made the insulting remark he was past the point of being apologetic and was responding in an equally hostile manner. There was no telling how the quarrel was going to be resolved, and whether it might escalate to punches being thrown or fizzle out. However, there is always someone who does not think things through.

One of the drunken men, who had not got involved up until this point, impulsively decided it was time he made a stand. He picked up a glass of beer and threw the contents wildly towards his target. It was, however, a bad shot. The drink went over his friend and the man he was aiming for, but also a number of innocent bystanders as well.

Vincent felt the cold beer splash against his neck and run down his back. He felt a familiar wave of anger course through him and he stood up to face whoever had thrown the beer. Just as he was about to engage with those responsible, a voice called out beside him.

"Vincent!" Barbara tried to get his attention from the other side of the bar. "Stop!"

Vincent stopped and turned to look at her. Barbara shook her head. As Vincent ran his hand down the back of his neck he could feel the stickiness of the liquid. Enraged, he faced his antagonists.

There was now a lot of shouting and pushing going on in the pub. No one was throwing punches and some of the men were holding others back from the fray. None of those involved had even realised there was a new threat to be aware of.

Vincent clenched his fists. He had done nothing to deserve this and was adamant that he should not let the incident go without reproach. It did not matter to him how many of them there were, there was no way he was going to be disrespected like that. But, as he stepped forward, he found his way blocked.

Barbara realised that her initial attempt to get Vincent to calm down had failed, so she had come around to the other side of the bar to intercept him. She now stood before him, creating a barrier between him and the trouble beyond. She had a determined and concerned expression on her face. "Come on, Vincent. It's not worth it. Don't do it to yourself," she almost pleaded. "Think about what could happen to you. Put yourself first. Don't let someone else force you into ruining your life."

Vincent regarded Barbara. She had his attention and he seemed to be focused on her rather than where the attack on him had originated. This was, at least, a start. As she continued her plea, Barbara gently put her hand on his chest.

"Give yourself sixty seconds. You owe yourself at least that. There are other people out there who won't even give you the time of day, so at least give yourself a minute. This is not you versus them. It's you versus you." Barbara could see that Vincent was still agitated so gave it one last shot. "There are two doors you can go through right now. One could see you in a prison cell and the other will mean you wake up tomorrow with your life still in your control. Do the right thing."

Vincent then looked round at the two girls he had been enjoying the night with. Unbeknown to him, the beer had gone over them also. They were now putting on their coats and about to walk out of the pub. A furious expression crossed his face as he turned towards the perpetrators.

The phone bleeped and the screen lit up. As a thumb swept across to reveal the text message that had just been received. It said everything that the recipient needed to know.

'I've got some great gear in if you're interested.'

Emma turned off the screen to hide the message, but it was too late. It had been seen by someone else. There would be no holding back.

"Oh my God, Emma!" Ryan's voice sounded astonished. "Who the hell is that?"

"Probably my old drug dealer. I'm not sure. The number didn't have a name." Emma appeared to be embarrassed and deflated. "I don't know why he's decided to contact me now."

"You've got to delete that message and block the number." Ryan made no attempt at trying to hide his disgust. "Don't let that bastard drag you down. He just wants your money. He doesn't care if he ruins your life."

At that point the phone bleeped again. This time Emma made no attempt to hide it. Another message appeared and they both read it at the same time. 'I've saved something extra special, just for you.'

"That makes me sick." Ryan showed nothing but revulsion at the message. "He's actually trying to make out he's doing you a favour. How can selling you that filth be beneficial?"

Emma was embarrassed. There was no way it could have been anyone else sending her a message like that. She had deleted her dealer's number months ago, but it seemed he had kept hers. That was a part of her life that she had tried her best to leave behind, but it now seemed to be following her.

Ryan's counselling session was about to begin. Most of the attendees were already there but he had seen Emma arrive and approached her for a chat. It was at that point the message had arrived.

"Do you mind if I bring this up with the rest of the group." He pointed to the other members. "It will be a lot easier with them supporting you as well."

Emma was not comfortable with this. It felt like she had let everyone down, even though she had done nothing. She could not have stopped that message from coming through, but she still felt responsible. Even though she would rather have kept it to herself, she knew sharing it with the group was the right thing to do.

"OK," she said reluctantly. "If you think it will help."

"It will. It definitely will." Ryan turned to face the rest of the group who were now all placing chairs into a circle into the middle of the room. "Right everyone, I've got something to tell you and I need your help."

At that the session began. The subject of Emma's text message was brought up straight away and everyone immediately offered their support. Some of the group told how they had received similar communications from their drug dealers, but had declined to engage. One of the members told them all how she had bought heroin when she had fallen into temptation, but had flushed it down the toilet thanks to her daughter's pleas. Every story was one of encouragement and motivation.

Emma listened to them all. It did not feel like she was fighting this on her own, and that felt really good. Battling against this was so much easier with so many people standing behind her. Unfortunately, none of them could stop what happened next.

While Emma was listening to the group exchanging stories of their struggles and trading words of inspiration she noticed something appear on her leg. There was a black spider on the tip of her knee. It was not huge, about the size of a penny. As it made its way along her thigh towards her waist, it almost seemed as though it had a predetermined destination. Inexplicably, it did. Of all the places it could have gone, it went into her pocket where her phone was. That was a cruel trick for her mind to play.

Everyone continued talking about their struggles and victories. It was a positive meeting. The group members had all felt the benefit and it was certainly one of the more beneficial discussions they had been a part of. There was, however, one exception.

Emma had sat there with a blank expression upon her face while everyone else had been talking. All she could think about was the contents of her pocket. So much was contained in that small space. It held her phobia and the means of dealing with it, yet at the same time her addiction and her mental health problems. For the remainder of the session, she kept her hand on her upper thigh as if to stop the demons from escaping.

When the meeting finally came to an end everyone said their goodbyes. A number of members came over to Emma to offer their support at this crucial moment, led by Ryan.

"You can call me at any time," he said. "You've got my number." His expression was sympathetic and his voice soothing. "If you have any problems with the way you feel or you're finding it hard to cope I'm available twenty-four hours a day. If the dealer contacts you again, block the number straight away. But you don't have to do this on your own. I'm here for you."

Emma knew she could talk to Ryan, or any of them, and they would unequivocally offer her their help. They were a good group of people and she really appreciated their support, but as she left, her hand was covering her pocket.

"Hello, we're your new neighbours. It's nice to meet you." A hand was offered along with the greeting. "I'm Alan, this is my wife, Sue, and this is our daughter, Wendy."

Oliver regarded the people in front of him. He did not speak, at first, but eventually responded to the offer of a handshake and made a feeble attempt to return the greeting.

"Hi, I'm Oliver." He felt awkward and it showed. "It's nice to meet you, as well."

At that, Alan nodded at the child beside him. Wendy looked at him inquisitively for a moment, but then a big smile crossed her face.

"We've got you a box of sweets." She lifted up the confectionary. "My favourites are the red ones."

Alan and Sue laughed at this. Oliver forced a smile, too, as he took the box from the girl. Although this was not an ideal situation he tried his best to be civil.

"Thank you very much." He opened the box and presented it to Wendy. "Why don't you take some of the red ones for yourself?"

There was no hesitation as the young girl planted her hand into the sweets and pulled out a fist full of her favourites. All three adults watched with grins on their faces.

"What do you say?" Sue prompted.

"Thank you!" said Wendy, unwrapping a red sweet.

Oliver looked back at the parents and nodded. "Thank you very much."

"It's good to meet you, Oliver." Alan replied over his shoulder as they left.

Oliver watched the young family walk up the garden path until they reached the end. He then closed the door and dropped the box of sweets on a table. That was not a situation that he wanted to find himself in.

As part of the conditions of his conviction, Oliver was legally obliged to inform the authorities if he found himself in contact with children on a permanent basis. This might include taking up work near a school or, as on this occasion, if he suddenly found he had minors move in near him. This situation had been forced upon him and he needed to deal with it.

As Oliver made his way upstairs he picked up a rag and can of glass cleaner that were on one of the steps. He had not cleaned his house in weeks and had only stopped halfway through his chores because the doorbell had sounded. When he walked into his bedroom he sprayed the windowpane and then prepared to wipe it. Something then caught his eye.

Oliver's semi-detached house was L shaped and so was his neighbour's that was connected to it. As he looked through the glass he could see directly down into the lower floor bedroom in the property opposite. Wendy was sitting on her bed eating sweets. This was not good.

"I've just got the usual questions before we begin." Gavin was filling in some forms as he spoke. "Have you got anything to report?"

Oliver hesitated for a moment. He was not too willing to divulge the information that he was required to, but knew he had no choice. If it was found out that he had withheld information from the authorities he could well end up in prison.

"Yeah! I've got new neighbours." He paused. "They've got a young daughter."

Gavin looked up from his paperwork. "Really? How old is she?"

"About four or five, maybe."

"Tell me everything."

Oliver had no choice but to describe the introduction that had taken place on his doorstep. No detail was left out and he even told Gavin that he offered the girl some sweets. He was completely honest and held nothing back.

"Well, I appreciate you being so forthcoming." Gavin had been making notes while he was listening and started to voice his observations. "You're going to have to make a few changes to counteract what has happened. For a start, you're going to have to move your bedroom to another part of the house, if possible. We're also going to have to inform the family that you are on the Sex Offender Register."

Oliver looked glum. He did not say anything. It was obvious what measures would have to be taken and he had expected them all. He would just have to suffer the constraints that were about to be put on his life.

Gavin could see that Oliver was downcast. He knew that the measures that were going to be implemented would have negative effects, but it was crucial that they were imposed.

"You've done the right thing, Oliver. This is better for everyone," said Gavin. "It's not only about you. It's about any potential victim as well. You remember how your father made you feel. We've got to make sure you don't do the same to someone else." Gavin leant forward in his wheelchair to stress the importance of what he said next. "If you feel the temptation to do anything illegal – anything at all – you must report it to me, no matter what. This is your chance to live a normal life."

Oliver did not respond.

It was twilight and the hall was dimly lit. The only illumination came from the streetlight outside. That was enough to be able to see.

Oliver tossed his keys and wallet on the table, next to the box of sweets. He then took off his coat and hung it on a hook on the wall. He then shuffled his way up the stairs to his bedroom. Once inside, he took out his phone to check his messages but couldn't help glancing across to his neighbour's house.

Everyone has a turning point in their life when they have to make an important decision. Most people make the right choice, whereas others do not. Those who choose the wrong path invariably regret it for the rest of their life.

    Leanne walked upstairs hand in hand with Bruno.

    Vincent lunged forward and threw a wild punch.

    Emma phoned her drug dealer and placed an order.

    Oliver took a photograph with the camera on his phone.

Many years passed and actions led to consequences. Leanne, Oliver, Vincent and Emma all paid a price for the decisions they had made. They had their chance to put things right, but they had failed, miserably.

Leanne's oldest son had not seen his father for eight years. Her two daughters, whom she had with her second husband, visited their dad at the weekends. She was currently pregnant with her latest baby while having a furious, ear-splitting argument with her most recent partner as the rest of her children looked on, scared and confused.

This was Leanne's life. It was a continual journey of going from one loveless fling to another, with nothing but heartache for everyone involved. Her children would regularly bear witness to the four relationship phases of introduction, idolisation, altercation and, finally, devastation. She had become both of her parents rolled into one.

All Leanne had ever wanted was to be loved. The problem was that, in order to get someone to love her, she needed to love herself. That was something she had never done. Every time she needed to show herself respect she abandoned her morals. She let people treat her terribly and, as a result, she never found what she was looking for. It was a shame that such a nice girl was always such a bitch to herself.

When Vincent had thrown the punch he had actually missed. What he had been unaware of was the man standing to the right of him who was looking out for his friend. He never saw the bar stool coming as it connected directly with the side of his head. No one ever accounts for the guy out of sight. It is that person who is the most dangerous.

It was inevitable that Vincent would end up in prison, but not one like this. The severe brain damage that he had suffered was what incarcerated him. His body was the cell walls and his mind the locked door, never to be opened again. Hardly anyone came to visit him at the nursing home, not that he was be aware of it when they did.

Vincent had been trying to fill a bottomless hole. It did not matter how many punches he threw he could not break free from the violence he had suffered as a child. His battle had not been with his stepfather, though, it had been with himself. Unfortunately, he had always fought the wrong person. The last punch he ever threw destroyed his life, and it had not even connected.

A blustery gale blew through Emma's hair as she stood at the top of the multi-story car park looking out across the town. As the wind got stronger the more it ruffled her clothes. The ferocious blast of air only stopped when she finally hit the concrete. Her body lay on the street below with every bone smashed.

Emma had abandoned her therapy and embraced her nemesis. The more she used drugs, the more her mental health deteriorated, so she used even more narcotics to suppress her visions and compulsions. It was not long until her mind was not hers anymore. All of her thoughts belonged solely to cocaine and, when she climbed over the barrier and threw herself off the edge of the car park it was barely even her who had made the decision.

There were plenty of people who were willing to talk to Emma about her problems and help her find the way out of the labyrinth that she had found herself in, but she chose to walk through the maze on her own. Every time she could have made a phone call or met up with someone who could help, she turned, instead, to the demon that had ensnared her. Just a confidential word about how she was feeling or an honest confession that she needed help with her addiction to a caring friend could have saved her. If someone, in a similar position had approached her for help she would never have turned them away. Unfortunately, she turned her back on herself.

It was peaceful in Oliver's room as he lay on the bed staring at the ceiling. Mind you, there was rarely anything happening around him these days. Not a lot does go on in an eight-by-twelve prison cell.

Oliver had once again been caught feeding his perversions and had been given a lengthy prison sentence. There was no second chance this time. He did not deserve one. When the police checked his computer the material they found on there was of a grade too awful for him to be trusted to live around normal people. He would be an old man when he got out.

Oliver had been a victim all his life. As a child, he had no choice but to be the recipient of his father's abuse and carry a terrible burden. That cumbersome weight stayed with him through to adulthood when the help of professionals could have reduced it, bit by bit, but instead he chose to offload it in its entirety on to other innocent people. That was the coward's way out. For that he would never be able to live a normal life again, just like his victims.

Leanne, Oliver, Vincent and Emma had destroyed their lives. All the damage had been done. There was nothing left for them now and there was no way back. It was over. As far as their lives were concerned it was quite simply…the end.

Chapter 8

There was total stillness in the room. No one moved and not a word was said. Everyone was utterly shocked by what had happened. Their thoughts were in turmoil. No one had expected that. It had ended so suddenly and brutally. This was not how things were meant to be.

Fortunately, there was one person present who was able to make sense of it all. She knew exactly what to say and how to say it. The uncertainty and confusion would not last for long. Mrs Reason spoke with her usual confidence and competence.

"So that's how their story ends, but how will yours end?" She sat at her desk at the front of the classroom, still holding the book. "All four of the characters in the novel had a dysfunctional home life. Whether it was due to violence, parents arguing, mental health issues, sexual abuse, or absent parents, they all had something going on that affected them in a negative way. As a result, they became adults who hurt others and themselves as well. They ruined their own lives because they carried the darkness of their past into their present and it determined their futures. When it was time to make a choice they made the wrong decisions and paid for it dearly. At some point in your lives, you will all have to choose a path to take. So what will you do?"

Mrs Reason paused to let her pupils think about the question. She knew it was important for them to absorb what she was saying. Leaving them to contemplate, she put the book on the desk and walked over to the window to look out across the school grounds. When she felt they had been given long enough to ponder the topic she carried on with the lesson.

"I should imagine that some of you associated yourselves with one or more of the characters in the book. Maybe you saw similarities between you and the boy who was a victim of violence. You might have mental health issues that meant you could relate to the girl who suffered from similar disorders. Of course, there's a strong possibility that you might not be affected in the same way as the individuals in the book. Violence doesn't always lead to violence, and mental health problems certainly don't always lead to drug addiction. However, maybe if your parents argue a lot, it has made you angry or prone to be aggressive. Your parents might both work, and you don't see them as much as you would like, or you may be from a single parent family, and this may affect your confidence and ability to socialise. There are all kinds of ways your life at home may not be perfect and many more ways that it could affect you. Mistreatment, violence, mental health issues, lack of attention and constant arguing can all lead to drug abuse, criminal behaviour, a lack of self-respect, depression, and other types of unacceptable behaviour. The point of this book is to identify what you are going through and how it is influencing you."

Mrs Reason raised a finger to stress the importance of her next point. "However, sometimes, someone else's home life might also affect you. If a person who you know is going through a hard time it may have an impact on you also. It might be a family member, a friend or someone who you are in contact with regularly, at school or work. They might bully you, they might annoy you unintentionally or they might even ignore you. So it's important to realise that this person is probably going through, or has gone through, an unhappy home life, which is why they are like they are. If one person bullies another person there are actually two victims; the one who is receiving the abuse and the oppressor who is likely to be going through some sort of torment of their own. It's as well to remember this if you find yourself being nasty to someone or someone is being unkind to you. The two of you will, almost certainly, have more in common than you realise."

Mrs Reason began to sum up the lesson. "So you might be experiencing problems in your life or someone you know may be going through a hard time. You might not be as happy as you want to be, or a friend may need your sympathy and understanding. That is why you need to identify what you are and what other people are. Are you happy or sad? Are they happy or sad? When you've done this you can start to deal with it.

"This brings us to our next question; do you want an easy life?" She did not wait for an answer, because she wanted to give it herself. "Because if you do, forget it. It's not going to happen. Life is hard. You're going to get ill, you're going to have unsuccessful relationships, you're going to end up in the wrong job, you're going to have toxic people in your life, and people close to you are going to die. So don't wish for an easy life, wish for the strength to handle a hard life, because that's what you're going to get. Don't look for a safe space when life gets hard, become a person who feels safe even when life becomes a hard. Yes, you will have some good times. A lot of good times, hopefully. And when you do, make sure you appreciate them, because you will certainly know when the bad times come around. You've got to reduce the harmful moments in your life, and the best way to do that is not to learn by your own mistakes, but to learn by other people's."

Mrs Reason started to walk amongst the desks, as was her custom. "People, places and points in time repeat themselves," she said in a clear voice. "There is someone just like you, somewhere else in the world, and they're the older version of you or the younger version of you. They made the same mistakes as you and they will make the same mistakes as you. They got the same things right as you did and they will get the same things right as you will do. We are all uniquely different, but there are many people out there who make the same mistakes as everyone else. The best you can hope for is to make as few mistakes as possible, and the best way to do that it to observe other people and learn by their mistakes. That can be anyone from your parents to peers or colleagues to friends. If you see someone regularly getting into fights and they get beaten up or put in prison, learn by it. When you hear about someone who has multiple sexual partners and does not use contraception, and they get pregnant at a young age or get a sexually transmitted disease, learn from it. There are plenty of people out there who have made big mistakes who you can learn from, so make sure you do. And, for goodness sake, don't be the person who other people are learning from. Don't be the drug user who becomes an addict, the gambler who loses all their money or the smoker who gets cancer. Be the person who gets it right and who others aspire to be like."

Mrs Reason had now, quite deliberately, reached the front of the classroom so that she could ask her pupils an important question. "But if you are going to learn about life, who do you think the best person to give advice to you is? Who can you trust to tell you to do the right thing? Is there anyone who you can believe one hundred per cent when they tell you what to do and what not to do?"

Mrs Reason waited for a show of hands, but none were raised. The pupils could have chosen family members, such as a parent or sibling, others might have chosen a best friend, but it appeared no one could actually think of someone who they could completely and utterly depend on. Fortunately, the answer was forthcoming.

"I'll tell you who you can trust to give you the best advice possible; who only wants the best for you and who is always close at hand: you. That's right, you. The point of this book is to make you think about what might happen to you if you make the wrong decisions. Rather than not knowing what's ahead, anticipate what might happen. Imagine how the characters in the book felt when their lives collapsed around them. Don't you think that they would have loved to travel back in time and do it all again? Imagine if that was you. Let's just say you've been caught breaking the law or you got into a relationship with a person you knew wasn't right for you. Wouldn't you love to go back with the knowledge you now hold and do it all differently? How great would it be to go back to when you were young and not do those things that ruined your life? Well, you can and you have. You're here now, able to put things right before they even went wrong."

"Standing before you right now is the future you, telling you not to do all those things that will wreck your life. You know you can trust the future you and you know they want the best for you. So what would they say to you? Would they tell you to work hard at school because you ended up poor? Would they tell you not to break the law because you ended up in prison? Would they tell you to respect yourself because you let yourself down? But would you take their advice? Would you tell them that they don't know what they're talking about? Would you ignore them? Would you think things are going to be different this time if you do the same things? Well, that future version of yourself knows more than you do. They've made your mistakes and don't want you to make them. The best advice you will ever get is from your future self, so don't disregard it. No one else wants more for you than you."

She summed up in her usual decisive manner. "So, think about what has happened in your past while you were a child, how it has affected you now and what you might do in the future. Think about the mistakes you might make and take steps to make sure you don't make them again. You must go full circle, all the way back to now. What are you going to do? How are you going to make things different? How are you going to live your life?"

Mrs Reason stood at the front of the class, looking at her pupils as they each pondered their future. Naturally, they all wanted to have good lives and hoped to have as few bad times as possible, but for a person to be motivated they must be repelled away from negative influences and attracted towards positive ones. The next part of the lesson would help with that also.

"So how happy do you want to be? Have any of you set yourself any goals? Maybe some of you want to get married and have children? Some of you might want to live in a nice house and have a good career? That is all fine, but if you want those things you've got to make sure you work to get them, and to do that you should set yourself a target to aim for.

"So let's say you set a score of one thousand to aim for and reach. I'll give examples of how you can do that. If you want a really nice partner, you've got to be a really nice person yourself, because if you want to get a great catch, you've got to be a great catch. So every time you're pleasant to someone give yourself a point. If you're nasty to someone take a point off, because a nice person won't like a nasty person. The higher your score goes the more likely you are to get the partner you want. If it drops too low you're probably going to end up in an unhappy relationship. And believe me, it happens.

"If you want that big house and good career, you could change your score to money. You might want to earn a thousand pounds a week. So every time you do your homework give yourself one penny. If you don't complete an assignment take one off. If you do really well in a test make it an extra five, or if you score low in an exam take five off. You can adjust these accordingly. This method of setting a target for yourself can help you in adulthood and it can be done in many ways. It might be a means of making yourself healthy, more knowledgeable or just plain happy. So set yourself goals and be honest with yourself when you do things right and when you get it wrong. Don't wait until tomorrow, because tomorrow never comes. The time to do something is always now. It's time to wake up. It's life-o'clock."

Mrs Reason drew two medium sized circles on the white board. Above the one on the left she wrote the words 'comfort zone', and over the one on the right she wrote 'discomfort zone'. She then stood sideways on so she could converse with the pupils and point to her graphical illustration.

"Everyone has two zones that they live in and an in between. We all have our comfort zone, which might be sitting down watching television in the evenings or playing computer games. There is also the discomfort zone which might be doing boring homework or tidying your bedroom. In between is neither of the two, like walking to get the bus or getting dressed in the morning. However, everyone's comfort zones differ in size." She scrubbed out both of the circles and made the comfort zone smaller and the discomfort zone bigger. "Let's say someone is unemployed and they get up at ten or eleven o'clock every day. One day they manage to get an interview for a job, but they have to get up at seven in the morning. This will be very hard for them as they are not used to it. Even though it's only a matter of getting out of bed, showering and making breakfast, it can put them in their discomfort zone. This is the same as someone who might never exercise, study or do overtime at work. When they need to run to catch the train, revise for an exam or put in extra hours to earn more money it is difficult for them. They spend too much time in their comfort zone and, as a result, it becomes smaller and smaller, whereas their discomfort zone becomes bigger and bigger. Simple tasks like getting to an appointment on time or being prepared for a project at school or work becomes hard for them."

Mrs Reason wiped away the circles and made the comfort zone bigger and the discomfort zone smaller. "Now if someone is used to getting up early in the morning, studying hard, exercising or working towards a goal all of those things become easy. Of course, when someone first starts going to a gym or learning about a new subject they begin in the discomfort zone, but the more time they spend there the easier it becomes. Their discomfort zone becomes smaller and their comfort zone becomes bigger.

"Needless to say, there will be times when you fall ill or suffer a family bereavement and you will find yourselves in your discomfort zone. It will never completely disappear, but it will become smaller and you find yourself in there only on rare occasions. So if you want lovely holidays in the sun or a nice house to live in, and don't want a low paid job or financial worries, make the effort to get out of our comfort zone, even if it means spending time in your discomfort zone. You'll find that life will get easier and the hard times will be few and far between. Make the effort."

Mrs Reason glanced at her watch and realised it was nearing the end of the school day. Although the study period was coming to its conclusion the lesson was not. The homework she was about to give would not be set out, or marked, by her, but instead would be administered by each of the pupils themselves. It would be down to them to carry out the assignment in whatever way they saw fit.

"I want you to take some time to think about your lives. Do it in the way that best suits you. You could discuss your feelings with family or friends. Tell them if you're unhappy, hurting or confused, if that's how you're feeling. If you are comfortable enough, tell them why you feel that way, what caused the problem and how it came about. Open up as much as you're prepared to. You will be surprised at how willing people are to listen to you. And if one of your friends wants to talk to you, listen. Don't just sit there thinking about what you're going to say next. Listen to what they're saying. And above all, care. Care about yourself, your friends and your family.

"When you come back on Friday I'm going to ask for volunteers to speak to the class about themselves. No one has to do it. It will be completely your decision. You can talk about your home life, your feelings, your future or whatever you like, whether it's positive or negative. Everyone here will just listen. No one will judge you or criticise you. I'm sure we will all have nothing but admiration for whoever gets up and talks to the class. It will show a great deal of strength to do so and whoever takes up the challenge should be extremely proud for being so brave. It's a hard thing to do to talk about personal things and open up about how you feel." Mrs Reason walked over to the door and opened it. "So that's your homework. Go find yourselves."

At that the pupils all began to file out of the classroom Mrs Reason followed them into the corridor. The noise of people shuffling feet quickly subsided. There were some individuals left behind in the classroom though; four, in fact.

"I don't know about you guys, but I could really associate with one of the characters in that book."

"Yeah, me too. I was actually thinking about myself when I was reading it, as though it was me who was going through it."

"I did that as well. I even gave the character in the book my name so that it was me I was reading about."

"When I realised that the story could be about me it scared me to think that I could go that way."

All four of them had been deeply affected by the book. They had so much to say to each other and even more to listen to. There was only one solution.

"Do you fancy going to the park?"

"Yeah."

"Definitely."

"Yup, OK."

At that, Leanne, Oliver, Vincent and Emma left the classroom.

It was a hot day in the park and it had attracted those who didn't have to work out of their homes to enjoy the sunny weather. A light scattering of clouds momentarily covered up the sun, granting the people below a reprieve from its beating rays, and a gentle breeze blew across the grounds, making the heat more bearable. It was as comfortable and tranquil as they could hope for, which was just as well for the four individuals lying in the middle on the grass. They had a lot to talk about.

Leanne, Oliver, Vincent and Emma lay on their backs, in their usual position, looking up at the sky. All four of them had a lot on their minds and each of them was contemplating what they were about to say. Previously they would have kept their problems to themselves, but things were different now. It would not be easy to talk about what was hurting them, or listen either, but they would all do their best for each other. This would be a significant moment in all of their lives, to lay their feelings bare and let the truth come out.

"I need to talk to you all about something." Emma sounded relaxed as she spoke. "If that's OK?"

"Yup, sure."

"Yeah, go for it."

"Go ahead."

"I've been having mental problems for a number of years now. It affects me quite badly at times. My mind makes me do things that I don't want to do and I see things that aren't there. It's really hard to explain, because I don't understand it myself. When I see numbers I have to add them up and subtract them. If I'm in a room that's got patterns on the walls or floor I have to make them into symmetrical shapes and count them. When I'm putting things like ornaments on a surface I have to make sure they're all straight and lined up. I have to do all of this, even though I know I don't need to, or want to, do any of it. Sometimes, I can switch it off, but most of the time I can't. It's called obsessive compulsive disorder, or OCD.

"The best way I can explain it is that it's like losing your phone. You spend ages looking for it, but you can't locate it. It's really frustrating, but you can't let it go. You can't relax until you know where it is. You just have to find it."

Emma closed her eyes to shut out the anguish, but carried on. "Occasionally, I see things that aren't there. It's normally caused by some kind of stress in my life, but not always. My mum works long hours to support us both and I am very lonely when I get home after school. My mind feels like a vast empty space and it's like my thoughts are stranded. That's normally when it happens. I see spiders a lot of the time. Some of them are small and others are big. They walk across my hands, tables and up walls. It's hard to tell whether they're real or not. There are other things I see as well, like cats sitting on fences or snakes lying alongside a wall. It feels similar to when you're dropping off to sleep and your mind creates random visions, like chairs, boxes and doors. Everyone does this when they are dozing off. The difference with me is that my mind does it when I'm awake, the things that I see are more regular instead of random and the hallucinations are more real. It's scary and I wish I could stop it, but I can't. I have to live with it. I'm not crazy. I'm normal. My mind just works differently.

"I wish I could talk to my mum about it, but she's always working. She has to. Everything is really expensive these days and she does all she can to pay the bills, but I wish that I could see her more. When she gets home she normally goes to bed because she's so shattered. She needs her rest. I get jealous when I see other children with their parents. It must be nice to hear someone tell you that you've done well in a test or that they're proud of you. I know my mum would love to say those things to me, but she can't. I love her and I know she loves me. We don't see enough of each other to show it. I wish it wasn't like this, but it is."

Emma's words came out in rush. No one else spoke. Those who were listening wanted to make sure that Emma had said everything that she wanted to before saying a word. This was her moment to get it all off her chest and her friends were more than willing to take the burden of the weight she was unloading. Sorrow shrinks quickly when generously shared.

"I've never told anyone about it before," said Emma. "It's kind of embarrassing. I know there's no immediate solution, but I needed to talk to someone about it, so I don't feel so alone. I know you must think it's weird and it's OK for you not to understand. I'm quite happy just to talk about it. In fact, I would like to."

The four friends then had a long conversation about Emma's mental health issues. A number of questions were asked and answered as best as they could be. No one was judgemental and none of them changed the subject to their own problems. They all concentrated on the topic at hand. A number of reassurances were offered.

Oliver was first. "You can always talk to us. If ever you want to meet up, at any place, at any time, just say."

"That's right, Em," said Leanne. "Don't think any of us are too busy or don't care. We all think the world of you and it won't ever be any trouble for us to give our time to you."

Vincent added, "You can phone us whenever you like, even if it's three in the morning. And if you're seeing things or your head is full of stuff or you're alone at home, let us know and we'll come around."

Emma took deep breath and closed her eyes. "Thanks guys. That means so much to me. Just having someone to talk to really helps a lot. And if any of you need me I'll be there for you too."

Again there was silence. Another of them used the moment to share their feelings.

"My parents argue. They argue a lot." Leanne stared straight up at the sky as her mind created pictures of her own thoughts. "It hurts terribly. I hate to see them so angry at each other. Their shouting deafens me. They say some really cruel things to each other, but their words hurt me more than anyone. I love them both, but I hate the way they make me feel. It's like I'm not there. They don't even notice me, let alone realise how sad they make me.

"When I fell over as an infant I would run to my dad or if I was ill I would cuddle my mum, but now it's them who are upsetting me I've got no one to turn to. I wish they knew how much it hurt. Maybe then they would stop. There are times I want to tell them how much pain they put me through, but it's so hard to do. I can't think of what to say to them. I don't even think they would listen. I sometimes wonder if I'll ever meet someone who will make me happy and care about my feelings. It would be so nice to have someone ask me how I feel, show that they care and who accepts me for being me, but I can't replace my parents. You can't substitute a parent's love and you can't expect someone to fill that void. No one wants to be a parent to an adult. I feel so lonely and lost. I just want to be loved."

A silence came over them, but there was no awkwardness. No one wanted to say anything without being completely sure that Leanne had said everything she needed to. They knew she really wanted to express her feelings and it was up to them to be listen. Words only have meaning if they are heard.

Leanne continued in a wistful voice. "I don't want to be with someone who might take advantage of my insecurities. There are people out there who prey on weak people. It's those people who I've got to avoid. I shouldn't give my love away too cheaply, but I am weak when someone gives me attention. That's why I need you guys. Sometimes, I can't do it on my own. Drag me away or tell me an uncomfortable truth, if that's what it takes."

There was no way that this was going to be ignored. The four then got into a discussion about the best way to help Leanne.

"There's no way I'm going to let someone take advantage of you, Leanne," said Vincent.

Emma nodded in agreement. "If you meet anyone who is even slightly out to hurt you I'll tell him and you what you both need to hear."

"You've got a lot of love to give, Leanne," said Oliver. "And there's someone out there who's going to be the luckiest person alive, but in the meantime you've got all of us looking out for you."

Leanne could not hide her happiness. "Thanks guys. I really appreciate it. It helps to know you've got my back. I'm there for you guys, too."

They each lay mulling over what was in their minds. There was no hurry to make conversation and they were all content to drift in and out of their own thoughts. When the time was right one of them decided to speak up.

"I can't tell you about my problems. I just can't." Oliver's voice was quiet and subdued. "I'm so unhappy, but I can't tell you why. I need help, but I can't ask you guys. I'm constantly hurting, but there's no painkiller that will work. It's not because I don't trust you all, because I do. I just have to sort things out on my own. There are times when I really need to get away from home and hang out with you all. Even if we talk about sport, music, television or whatever else, that's fine. Anything to take my mind off things is helpful. I need to feel normal. Even feeling OK is enough for me. There are times when I'm quiet and locked away in myself, but that's just how I need to be at that time. Don't be offended if I don't want to talk about it. Being with you guys to take my minds off things is better than being alone. I wish I could tell you why I am sad sometimes, but all I ask is that you understand you all being there for me is enough. I really appreciate your friendship. I wish I could say more, but I can't."

No one asked Oliver to say more. The message understood. Sometimes the loudest cry for help is spoken with the softest words.

"One day I hope that I won't be this way," Oliver said longingly. "I know my past will always be a part of me, but I will do my best not to let it affect me. My life is mine to live and no one else's. Maybe at some point in the future I will tell you everything, but that can't be now. I need your patience and understanding."

None of Oliver's friends pressed him to say more and were happy to let him reveal as much as he wanted in his own time.

Leanne was the first to offer her support. "You don't have to tell us anything that you don't want to. This is not about us, it's about you."

"You're not alone, Ollie," said Emma. "No matter how long it takes for you to sort it out we'll be here for you."

Vincent added, "If there's anything you need you know who to ask. There's nothing that we won't do to help for you."

Oliver swallowed hard, choking down his emotions as he showed his gratitude. "Thank you. Thank you, all of you." He felt overwhelmed. "I won't let any of you down either."

Yet again they all lay quietly, enjoying the warm sun. Each of them felt at ease in each other's company and the silence was not uncomfortable. They could have stayed laying there for ages, but one more of them needed to speak.

"This is not easy for me. It's not easy at all. I find it really hard to talk about myself. It makes me feel weak." Vincent steadied himself and then said, "My stepfather hits me. He hits me all the time. Sometimes I do things wrong, but nothing that terrible. He's just got a really bad temper. He rarely works and drinks a lot, so he's got no money. That makes him angry. Sometimes he doesn't even bother trying to find a reason to hit me, but other times he makes something up. The washing up's not done, something has been spilt on the carpet or a window has been left open, are all used as reasons to punch me. I cover up the bruises or lie about them. Long sleeve shirts in the summer and black eyes from playing football. They're just different lies to hide the same truth; that I'm a victim of abuse.

"My mum doesn't do anything to stop it. I know she's scared; scared of being hit herself and of being alone if she was to leave him. I don't blame her, but at the same time I wish she'd do something. I know she loves me, but she's not strong enough to show it. Of course it hurts physically, but the worse thing is how it makes me feel. It's not just the unhappiness, but I'm angry as well. I'm always angry. Sometimes, I feel like the only way to stop the pain is to hit someone to make myself feel better. It's like if I look down on someone else I won't feel so low. If I make someone else my victim, then maybe I won't be a victim anymore. But that's not the person I want to be and I know that won't stop what I have to put up with at home. I feel so down. I don't want to live like this."

The three friends had great admiration for Vincent. They knew how hard it had been for him to say all of that. He was physically strong, but to show such mental strength and reveal such vulnerability had been inspiring. There is no muscle mightier than the mind.

"I don't want to be like my stepfather," said Vincent determinedly. "I want to be me. I need to be me. At some point in my life I'll move away from him and when that happens I can't bring who he is with me. That's not going to be easy, because I'll still be angry, but I'm doing my best to control it. That's why I need you guys. If you see me about to do something that's going to get anyone hurt, you stop me. Whether you try to calm me down or need to be critical, I want you to tell me what I need to hear. All that matters is that I don't screw my life up or anyone else's. I'm not too proud to ask for help."

Such a strong person asking for strength from others was rare, but Vincent knew he could rely on his friends. They discussed his difficulties and ways to deal with them in future. At no point did he feel depreciated or without hope. Their offers of support were heartfelt.

"We all know how strong you are, Vincent, but with us by your side, you'll be even stronger," said Emma.

"There's no shame in asking for help," said Oliver. "It's not weakness. It shows strength."

Leanne added, "You're the toughest person I know. The fact that you're willing to talk about such things proves it."

Vincent's heart filled with pride. "You guys are great. You really are." He nodded in agreement. "There's no way I'll let any of you down."

The four friends felt much better after having an opportunity to discuss their problems. To actually be able to talk about what was on their minds had helped them relieve a huge burden. No one had interrupted while each of them had been talking and they had all listened carefully to every word that had been spoken. None of them had mocked, undervalued or judged what the others had had to say. They had shown only compassion, admiration and encouragement. Together they were much more resilient, decisive and focused.

When dusk came they left the park together and made their way back to their homes. Each of them felt an element of pride in themselves, not just for having the strength to talk about the difficulties in their lives, but for also responding when asked to carry the weight of each other's burdens. This had been beneficial to all of them and the affect it would have on their lives would be immeasurable. They were not just friends, but towers of strength that each of them could lean upon when needed.

Leanne walked into her bedroom and opened up her laptop. Within minutes she had found the online content that she had been searching for. She spent the rest of the evening studiously reading and feverishly writing.

Oliver puts his keys, wallet and phone on the cabinet in the far corner of his room. As he did so, his father, Brian, appeared at the doorway. This had been expected.

Vincent strolled into the living room and gazed at his stepfather who was asleep on the sofa. He shook his head as he eyed all of the empty beer cans scattered on the floor. The expression on his face was one of pity.

Emma was in the kitchen, looking at the refrigerator. Attached to it were a number of business cards from the places of employment where her mother worked. In the top corner, however, was a card for the local restaurant where, on rare occasions, the two of them would go together. It was this that had her attention.

Chapter 9

Leanne, Oliver, Vincent and Emma walked into the classroom and stood by their desks. They looked at each other and smiled. Their confidence was high and they each had a newfound optimism in their lives. Everything seemed so much clearer now they were aware of who they were and who they eventually wanted to be.

The rest of the pupils ambled into the classroom, and Mrs Reason followed them. She waited for them all to sit down and settle before starting the lesson. When she was sure that everyone was focused she began.

"OK, as you all know, last lesson I asked if any of you wanted to talk to the rest of the class about your lives. Of course, no one has to do it and whoever does can talk about whatever they like. No one will judge you and everyone will listen." She looked across the classroom. "Who would like go first?"

Mrs Reason did not expect any of the pupils to enthusiastically put themselves forward. Public speaking is never easy, especially if the subject matter is personal. Nevertheless, a hand was raised amongst and the first volunteer appeared to be quite eager.

"OK, Emma. Go ahead." Mrs Reason was clearly pleased. "Begin in your own time. And well done."

Emma stood up and walked to the front of the classroom. Her classmates looked at her expectantly. She showed no hint of nervousness and she seemed to be confident. When she began to speak it was in a precise and positive way.

"I have mental health problems. I'm not ashamed of it and I'm not embarrassed by it. It's hard for me to understand it and even harder to explain it, but I will do my best. I have two conditions that affect me. I have obsessive compulsive disorder, known as OCD, and I suffer from psychosis. These both sound confusing, and that is why mental health awareness is such a problem. It has been made too complicated by the medical profession.

"I'll give an example: if you receive treatment for mental health problems you might be given something called CBT, which stands for cognitive behavioural therapy. That itself sounds too complex. A parent whose child suffers from mental health issues might feel excluded from the treatment because it sounds so difficult to understand, but CBT is simply when a counsellor gets the patient to change their thoughts in order to change their behaviour. That's it. I believe the problem with solving mental health issues is that it's made too complicated. If someone breaks their elbow the doctor doesn't tell them they've got an intercondylar fracture to the cubitus, because it's too hard to understand. They just tell the patient they've got a broken elbow. That's what needs to happen with mental health.

"Instead of illnesses of the mind being referred to as psychosis, schizoaffective disorder or body dysmorphic disorder, I feel they should more commonly be referred to as something simple like a 'bruised mind', 'broken brain' or 'fractured thoughts'. Everyone can then relate to the problem more easily. We've all fallen over and grazed ourselves and some of us have broken a bone. It's no different with the mind. Just because there's no plaster it doesn't mean there's no pain. Sometimes the brain gets injured and it doesn't work properly. You wouldn't ask a person with a broken leg to run a marathon, so why expect someone with a broken mind to walk through life unaided?

"The reason people don't associate physical impairment with mental impairment is because if someone has an injured limb you can see the damage, but when the brain is injured you can't see the wound. But the brain is like an egg. It changes on the inside. With an egg the embryo grows and turns into a developed life form. It's no different with the brain; its structure changes on the inside. It goes through a process called neuroplasticity, which basically means it alters in its structure; no different to an egg. What people with mental health problems need is for others to identify with that. A mind that doesn't work is no different to a hand that doesn't hold or a knee that doesn't bend. We need people to understand us. We just need a bit of help. And the great thing about that is that it's really easy to do most of the time. All you have to do is listen to us, try to understand us and realise that we're no different to any of you. We just have something wrong with our minds as opposed to something wrong with our bodies."

Emma pointed a finger at her chest. "So I'm going to explain what's wrong with me. As I mentioned before, I have OCD, but we're going to refer to it as simply 'brain chores'. It affects me in a strange way. I have to keep doing the same pointless things over and over. If I see numbers I have to subtract, divide, multiply or add them up. When I see patterns I have to line them up, count them or try to make them symmetrical. I also have to put things like pens and pencils on a desk so that they all line up. Sometimes, I find myself spending a long time looking at wallpaper or arranging ornaments on a shelf for no reason. It's hard to ignore or suppress the urges to do all of this, but I've found that the best way to fight it is to try to concentrate on something else, like counting the coins in my pocket."

"As for my psychosis, we'll call that 'mind lies'. My brain lies to me and I see things that aren't there. Normally, I see spiders, but sometimes I also see animals. I suffer from arachnophobia, a fear of spiders, which makes it even worse. Sometimes they're big and on other occasions they're small. It normally happens if I'm feeling nervous or uncomfortable. It's not nice seeing spiders crawling up my arms or legs. In fact, there are spiders all over the floor of the classroom right now."

This was met with grimaces from some of the pupils. One or two of them even lifted their feet off the ground. Emma smiled and carried on with her explanation.

"I try to tell myself that they're not there and everything is fine. That doesn't always work though, but it's nice when it does. Whether I'll rid myself of these mind illnesses, I don't know, but I've come to accept that it's part of who I am. It's good to talk to people about it and not try to hide it. No one should be ashamed of having a bruised brain or broken mind, just as no one should be embarrassed about having a sprained ankle or bad back. We're all human and we all get ill. None of us are without weakness, and the strongest people are the ones who fight the biggest battles. My conflict is with myself. That is who I am; a mental health sufferer who is winning every day."

Emma felt proud of herself. To have actually told a classroom of pupils about her mental health problems was no easy task and she had done it flawlessly. The round of applause from her peers confirmed that.

"Well done, Emma." Mrs Reason was impressed. "That was excellent."

Emma walked back to her desk and sat down. She glanced at each of her close friends in turn, who all smiled at her approvingly. That felt really good.

"Who wants to go next?" Mrs Reason scoured the classroom for a volunteer.

Vincent did not even put his hand up. He just got to his feet and walked to the front of the classroom. His determination and resolve were evident.

Mrs Reason did not question the pupil standing next to her. She realised that he had made a few small steps in order to take larger ones. This was fine by her.

Vincent was composed as he spoke. "I'm angry. I'm always angry. My stepfather is also angry, so he passes it on to me. My home life has made me this way. It's not how I want to live my life. I don't want to get into fights. I don't want to be hated or hate myself. I've got to make sure that I don't use my anger as an answer to my problems. Life is not about how hard you hit, but about how well you can take a hard hit. Everyone has, and will have, bad times throughout their life. There's no avoiding that. What matters is how you handle it and how you get up after you've been knocked down.

"I know things will happen to me that will really make me furious, but when those times come I've just got to say one word so that I don't make things even worse for myself. That word is 'stop'. Everyone should use that word when they're about to do something that could affect them or someone else in a bad way. Give yourself some time to think about what about to do. Weigh things up and work it out. I don't believe that people can't control their temper. In fact, I think people deliberately lose their temper. You never see a person on their own try to fight seven big men, but how many times do people pick a fight with one person weaker than them? That's what cowards do. Bullies think that they get away with it every time they pick on someone, but they don't. The law of averages says that they will get their comeuppance one day. They might go to prison or hospital, or even worse they'll hurt someone close to them. If you end up losing one of your family or friends, you're only harming yourself. That's no way to live. Life is hard, but you've got to learn to deal with it. I don't want to be a loser. I don't want to be a fool. I want people to respect me because I treat them right. That's real respect." He shrugged his shoulders. "That's all I've got to say."

Again the class applauded. Vincent could not help smiling. It had been hard for him to be so humble, but it felt good to get it all out into the open. It takes strength to reveal your weaknesses.

"Well done, Vincent," said Mrs Reason. Once again, she addressed her pupils. "Anyone else?"

Oliver put his hand up. After getting a nod of approval from his teacher he made his way up to the front of the class. For a moment he stood looking at all the faces staring back at him. He then began.

"My life is not normal. I wish it was, but it isn't. If it was normal I could describe it to you, but it isn't so I can't. Normal is underrated. Average gets a bad rap. Ordinary doesn't get the respect it deserves. Things happen to you in life that can destroy you and there's nothing you can do to prevent it. A family member might get seriously ill or even die. You could get a terminal illness yourself or you could end up with a serious disability. When something like that happens you'd give anything for things to be normal. If you've been through hell, normality is heaven. When you've hit rock bottom, halfway up feels like the top of the mountain. When all you've known is pain, feeling numb is a pleasure. All I want is normality. It's something that's worth aiming for, because if you're going to take a fall from a great height, no one ever misses the ground. So when the time comes to make the right decision for yourself you've got to do it no matter what. It will rarely be easy and it will probably be extremely hard, but it will always be worth it. When you need to change your life don't let your voice be a quiet whisper; let it be a lion's roar. Don't settle for anything less than you deserve, need or want. That's what I've got to do for my sake and everyone around me. So in years to come if I've achieved normality I will have got everything I wanted in life. If you see me queuing in a supermarket, that's fine. If you see me working in a nine-to-five job, that's great for me. If you see me with an average family, it means I've overachieved." He timidly hugged himself. "Normal is the new fantastic."

A round of applause filled the classroom. Oliver grinned shyly as he made his way back to his desk. Each of his close friends smiled at him.

"That was very good, Oliver." Mrs Reason looked around the classroom. "Does anyone else want to talk?"

Leanne put her hand up while holding a piece of paper. She immediately received a gesture from her teacher to proceed. At the front of the classroom, no time was wasted and she got straight to it.

"In the book we are studying, one of the characters refers to a letter written by Oscar Wilde called 'De Profundis'. She said that it changed her life, so I decided to read it myself. I found it online. It really is excellent. It's sad, but really deep and meaningful. So it got me thinking about me and my future self. I started to wonder what my life will be like if I make the wrong decisions. There might be times when I need advice and support. So I decided to write a letter myself, but not to anyone else; to me. I wrote it so that the person I am now can help the future me make the right decisions. That's what I'm going to read to you all now. I've also called it De Profundis, because it's from the depths of my heart." She lifted up the piece of paper in her hand and began to read.

"Dear Leanne, I have decided to write to you myself, as much for your sake as for mine, as I would not like to think that you would pass through however many years of your life without receiving a single line from me. There's almost certainly a lot we could say to each other. You can probably look back at all of the mistakes that I will make and that you have made. I hope that there's not too many and they're not too bad. If I have done something you regret, please forgive yourself and do not make things worse by making the same mistake again. I know I will not have been perfect, but I'm sure I won't have ruined your life either. I should imagine that right now you're considering doing something you and I might regret at a later date. That is why you are reading this letter, and as you know, that is why I wrote it. Even if this is the hundredth time you have read it, please carry on. I am sure I do not need to remind you that when you wrote this you meant every word.

"So let's get down to the problem at hand. If you've met someone and you suspect that they might hurt you, please walk away. If you saw him chatting up someone else before he turned his attention to you, do not take the risk. If he has a reputation, do not become a part of it. I know you, Leanne. I know you better than anyone. I know what you're thinking. Of course I do, I am you. You'll be telling yourself 'he is not that bad', 'people don't understand him' and 'he makes me feel so good about myself'. You're lying to yourself. Stop! Just stop it! All the feelings you have for him are created by you, not him. I know it is not easy for you. You want to be loved. We have always wanted to be loved. But love is only worth having if it's the real thing. And we both know that's not what he's offering you. Bitches and bastards finish first with bitches and bastards. Don't be a bitch! Respect yourself.

"Don't treat yourself in a way that you would never treat someone else. Be as kind to yourself as you are to others. Have confidence in yourself. You and I both know what you're capable of. You are wonderful. There is no man out there who is capable of getting a better girlfriend than you. Whoever they are, they are worth waiting for. If you know a good person, be a good person and take them for yourself. Finish first. Because that's what good girls do; they finish first with the good guys. If the good guy is a bit boring, maybe he's just shy. If you get to know him he might make you laugh when you are low, cuddle you when you are cold, or cheer you up you when you're sad. Give him a chance. He might have written a letter like this too. He might be looking for a good person who can offer him real love. He might be waiting for you. This might take some time, but it will be worth it. There will be times when you are in the gutter, looking for the stars on a cloudy night, but those clouds will eventually clear. And when they do, you can enjoy the light of those distant suns once again. Be patient. Your time will come. We both know that love is what will give you happiness in life. Settle for nothing less than one hundred per cent. Hopefully, one day, you won't need to read this letter again. You'll be so happy enjoying your present and looking forward to our future. You won't need to think of the past. You will have someone who cares deeply for you, because you will care deeply for yourself, just like I do. I know this will happen. You know what you must do for us both. We are one. Your mistakes are my failures, as my mistakes have been yours. Although this letter was written by me, it has always been about you. You read this letter to learn the pleasure of life and love. Perhaps I can teach you something much more wonderful, about you and your beauty. Your loving self, Leanne."

All the pupils in the class applauded loudly. Leanne did not want to remain the centre of attention for too long so quickly made her way back to her desk. As she sat down, each of her close friends beamed at her proudly. She felt great and they felt great for her.

"That was excellent, Leanne." Mrs Reason looked up at the clock on the wall. "It's almost lunchtime now. You can use the remaining few minutes to talk amongst yourselves."

The pupils spent what was left of the lesson chatting to one another. When the school bell sounded they all got up and left, apart from the four good friends. They remained seated, chatting to each other. Mrs Reason approached them and sat down on a neighbouring chair.

"Thank you, you four. You taught the class for me today. That was courageous and impressive. I know it wasn't easy, but you did really well. I'm extremely pleased for you all."

Vincent was the first to respond. "Thank you, as well, Mrs Reason."

"Yeah, thanks for giving us the chance to talk about things," said Emma.

"These lessons have been really helpful," Oliver added.

Leanne summed up all their feelings. "Thanks for everything you've done for us, Mrs Reason. We really appreciate it."

Mrs Reason smiled proudly. It was a job well done for her. Although teaching was her profession, it was more of a passion. Nothing felt as good as seeing her pupils make something out of their lives. This was the real payment for her services.

Chapter 10

The music from the party carried across the streets. The sound of excited teens, laughing and joking, could also be heard as they descended from all directions on the large red house where the party was being held. There was only one place to be tonight.

As they got closer, they could feel the base vibrating. Some were wearing designer clothes, others smelt of cologne and had waxed hair. They all carried bags, several of them containing spirits and mixers. Most people from school were going. Tommy Doyle's parties were legendary.

Leanne, Oliver, Vincent and Emma stood outside chatting.

"This is going to be interesting evening," said Leanne. She glanced around at her friends.

"You're not wrong. I've heard someone's bringing some drugs."

"Yeah, and watch out for people trying to spike your drinks."

"You just know some idiot will start a fight."

"And there's bound to be the usual losers bragging about their conquests."

"Yeah, well, that's down to them."

All four of them felt resolute and confident. They knew they could rely on each other for support, but they were also aware that, at times, they would have to fight their own battles. None of them were alone, but they were all prepared to face whatever life had in store for them. This knowledge was moulded out of an individual and collective strength.

They were out to have a good time tonight, even though they were wary of any pitfalls. As they entered the house, one of them hung back.

"I'll meet you there." Vincent stood there in an isolated pose. "I've got to sort something out first."

The other three stopped and turned to face him. Vincent obviously had something that he wanted to deal with on his own. None of the others questioned him.

"OK."

"We'll see you there."

"Be careful."

Leanne, Emma and Oliver disappeared inside Vincent walked off towards a side street.

The alleyway was mostly dark, but at the far end a welcome glow emanated from a streetlight. Some might have found it daunting to walk down the alley alone, but the young man walking purposefully through it right now was not fazed by such things. He had a sturdy build and tough demeanour. This was not the sort of person who could be easily victimised.

Josh Hanger ambled along to the party. He had not received a direct invitation, but no one would have dared tell him his presence was not wanted. Most people were hoping he wouldn't turn up. Even his friends were not that keen on him.

As Josh reached the end of the alley, someone appeared out of nowhere, blocking his way. At first, he could not see who it was and he squinted to get a better view of them. This was not a comfortable feeling, even for someone as robust as him. It was only when the person stepped into the glow of the streetlight that their identity was revealed.

"We need to talk." Vincent's face was now well lit. "We need to sort this out."

"You're right, we do," Josh snarled, adopting a combative stance. "We need to sort this out right now."

Vincent continued. "There's no point in causing a ruck in front of everyone else with other people getting involved. It needs to be just you and me, face to face." He put his arms out to his side and showed his palms in a yielding posture. "But I don't want to fight you. That's not what I'm here for."

Josh was perplexed. He had been convinced he was being ambushed, but now it appeared otherwise. If he had found himself in a fight, he would have gone into his usual rage, but instead he was curious. He was not sure what was more uncomfortable; being punched in the head or made to think.

Vincent took a step forward, but not in a hostile manner. "I know you threw that ball at me on purpose. You were looking for trouble. Well, you found it, because I wanted a fight as well. Confrontation doesn't scare me. It wouldn't even matter to me if you hit me. I get that enough at home. Just one more punch to the face or kick to the ribs is not going to break me. But getting into a fight with you could ruin my life, whether I win, lose or draw. I'm not about to do that to myself. I've seen what a life of violence does to people and it's not for me. My stepfather is a brutal bastard and a drunken loser. He makes no attempt to control his anger and hits people for no reason, including me. He's got nothing in his life and that's not how I want to end up. So the way I see it is: if you don't like them, don't be like them."

Josh stared at Vincent as he considered his words. He hadn't expected this. In fact, he had not anticipated any of it.

"So… What… Your stepfather hits you?" He appeared confused by this. "Why… What's that about?"

Vincent described his life morosely. "My stepfather is always out of work, so he's rarely got any money. That makes him unhappy, so he drinks. That eats away at what little money he has left, so that makes him angry; and so he takes it out on me. He'll hit me for anything; a punch to the face for not getting him a beer or a kick on the shin for being in the way.

"You're not the first person this week to want to hit me. If you and I were to fight you could probably hit me as hard as my stepfather does, but I could possibly hit you just as hard. Neither of us would win. We'd both end up as bruised as each other, but still as angry as we were before. There's a reason why you tried to pick a fight with me and it's probably got something to do with your home life as well. We're both angry and want to take it out on someone else, but what will that achieve?

"We don't really know each other, but if anger is all we've got in common that shouldn't be a reason to bash the hell out of each other for everyone else's amusement, because you know there are people at that party tonight who would love to see us fight. I'm not going to be their entertainment and I don't think you want to be either. So it's up to you how this goes, Josh."

The two stood facing each other. It was a close quarter stand-off that meant if one of them was to throw the first punch the other would have little chance of avoiding it. They were at each other's mercy. It all came down to who would be the first to react.

"You've got some balls, facing off with me," said Josh. "Not many people would do that and walk away without getting punched." He half smiled. "I respect that. And you're right; people would like to watch us go at each other. Why should we be their entertainment? My dad used to hit me, too, right up until the point he walked out on us all. So, yeah, I'm angry all right."

Josh reached out his hand and it was taken up by Vincent. They were both relieved not to be caught up in a vicious brawl and it showed in their grateful expressions. Although the two of them would have fought ferociously if necessary, both would rather walk away unscathed. No one likes being punched, especially before a party.

Vincent looked up the road in the direction of the party. "Well, there's no point in us missing out. Imagine how much everyone would miss us."

"Yeah, because I'm really well-known for my amusing banter," said Josh.

As they made their way to the party they spoke about their lives at home, how it had affected them and how they felt. They were actually similar in a lot of ways; two broken souls wanting to piece themselves together instead of smashing each other to bits. That was something worth fighting for.

Anger and violence featured in both Vincent's and Josh's lives, but tonight it had been suppressed. Not only that, the imminent threat had started an unlikely friendship. A close friendship, born from the ashes of hostility, that would continue to burn for many years to come. These two flames would never scorch each other now, but would instead light the way for one another.

The main hub of the party was the large living room. This was where the DJ was blasting out the latest tunes. It was full of youngsters dancing and appeared to be the best place to be. The atmosphere was electric.

Leanne, Oliver, and Emma had been there for a while and had only just been joined by Vincent. They were happy to watch the other partygoers, while having a drink, from the sidelines. They would get involved later, but none of them had any inclination to get caught up in anything that might be detrimental to them.

Now and then someone would approach the group for a chat and each of them would talk for a while. Josh Hanger had walked past, at one point, but any flicker of trouble was soon extinguished when he gave Vincent a high five. The evening was going well. It was only until a voice sounded to the side of Leanne that the mood changed.

"I'm glad you came." Brad Jacobs stood there with his well-practised smile. "I was starting to wonder if I was going to be bored by the usual people all night. It's about time someone interesting turned up."

Leanne glanced around at her friends. Their expressions were full of suspicion, but she had been expecting this.

"Hey, why don't we go over there?" Brad was eager to get his prey away from the protection of the herd. "We can have a quiet chat. Get away from the crowd."

At that, Brad led Leanne by the hand towards the dining room which was much less occupied. She did not resist, but she did not appear enthusiastic either. As they walked, he tried his best to keep eye contact with her, but she didn't seem that eager to do likewise. When they came to stop by the large table in the centre of the room he put both of his hands on her waist, but again she did not respond. This was not what he had anticipated.

It did not take long for Brad to start wielding his silver tongue. He dished up all of his best chat-up lines. He kept his eyes fixed on his conquest, and his hands wandered up and down Leanne's back. It wouldn't be long before they could move the action to the bedroom. At least, that's what he thought.

Leanne had been listening to every word, but was taken in by none of it. She noticed that a few of Brad's friends had gathered in the doorway and were watching him closely. They were obviously expecting another impending triumph that would be boasted about in the coming weeks. Leanne had no intention of becoming the subject of gossip tonight.

"Are you expecting me to sleep with you?" Leanne asked directly.

Brad was taken aback by the suddenness of the question, but quickly came to his senses. "Well, if that's what you want, I won't turn down you down."

"…because it's not going to happen."

Leanne nodded in the direction of Brad's friends. "So are you going to tell your mates that I turned you down because I'm a lesbian or frigid?"

"No, of course not." Brad's cheeks flushed. "I'd never lie about you."

"Good. Then go and tell your friends that I turned you down because you're a complete prick."

At that, Leanne turned away, leaving Brad wounded and bleeding. Leanne rejoined her friends. They all noticed how happy she was. They had all been willing to give her their support if she had needed it, but she had done it on her own. If you do not fall down you do not need anyone to help you back up.

The party was still going strong and a number of teenagers were now more drunk than they had probably intended. Some were asleep on the floor, whereas others could hardly stand up. Peculiarly, the people who were the most awake were those who had gathered at the top of the house, huddled around a bathroom.

Emma had left her friends to top up her drink and then decided to see what was going on upstairs. As she made her way up the large staircase she squeezed past a number of partygoers who seemed oblivious to her presence. When she finally reached the top she received an unexpected whip round the face.

"Sorry!" The apology was given instantly and without hesitation. "I didn't see you there."

Kim Warnock had been trying unsuccessfully to wrap her scarf around her neck, but in the process had lashed Emma around the face with it. Even now she was trying to twist and turn the garment so that it fit her perfectly. It all appeared to be rather clumsy and pointless.

Emma rubbed her stinging eye as she watched Kim struggling to fit the scarf around her neck in a manner that she found acceptable. She kept undoing it and then making another unsuccessful attempt to reapply it, even though there was little wrong with it in the first place.

"Are you OK?" Emma asked in a concerned voice. "Let me help you with that."

At that she took hold of the scarf and wrapped it once around Kim's neck. It fit perfectly. No ruffles and no twists.

"Thank you." Kim smiled sheepishly. "I struggle with things like this. I find it hard to coordinate at times. Silly, isn't it?"

"No worries. None of us are perfect." Emma smiled. "We all need a hand occasionally."

"You're probably right. I take too long to do things sometimes. The doctors say I have Asperger Syndrome. They say that it makes me want to match things up that don't need to be. That's why I was fidgeting with my scarf. It's tartan and my coat's got squares on it. Weird, eh? It's not all bad though. I'm really good at remembering things. I know every song that's got to number one in the charts for the last three years and I know all the names of the dungeons in Skyrim. The music is a bit too loud for me. That's why I'm upstairs. It gets inside my head and it won't come out. Light does that as well. I'm not too good at talking to people and things like that. I sometimes keep talking without thinking about what I'm saying. I can go on for hours. I suppose I'm doing that now. I'm keeping you from where you want to be, aren't I? Sorry, you probably want to get going."

Emma looked towards the bathroom. There were a handful of people standing outside and a few more inside. She could see a girl bending over the sink and who seemed to be sniffing something.

"I'd rather talk to you." Emma put a friendly hand on Kim's shoulder. "Why don't we go down to the floor below? It's not too loud there either and you can tell me about Asperger Syndrome. I find that sort of thing really interesting."

Emma and Kim went downstairs and spent the rest of the evening talking about themselves and their problems. Their mental health issues were discussed in full and how it affected their lives. They even spoke about how hard it was to speak to other people about it and get them to understand. It was comforting for both of them to talk so openly with someone who had experienced similar difficulties. No one is truly alone in a world where so many people are the same.

The party was coming to an end. All that was left was a large mess of empty bottles and glasses, spilt drinks and vomit stains. A few teenagers were crashed out on the sofas and on the floor. It had been a great night; not that everyone would be able to remember it.

Oliver had spent most of the evening with his best mates, but was tired and had now decided to leave. He had left his hoodie in a room upstairs and was endeavouring to find it. He was walking along the landing, trying to remember which room he had left it in. Noticing a door to a room that had been left ajar and uncertain whether this was where he had been earlier in the evening, he peeked inside. Lying on a bed in the middle of the room was a girl wearing a very short skirt.

Oliver peered up and down the corridor to see if anyone was around. There were two guys at one end who both appeared to be extremely drunk and were clumsily staggering about. It looked like they had lost all of their inhibitions.

Oliver took a step inside. He left the door half open so that enough light could enter into the room. He recognised his hoodie amongst a heap of coats on a chair in the corner.

A noise came from outside. It sounded like something had been knocked over. Oliver assumed that it had been caused by one of the drunken teenagers and became concerned that they were making their way towards the room that he was in. It was time to act. He grabbed a coat from the pile and covered the lower half of the girl. She would not be mistreated tonight.

Satisfied that he had prevented any immediate possibility of the girl attracting unwanted attention he grabbed his hoodie. As he pulled it over his head, he started to walk quietly out of the room.

"Who's that? Who's there?" The girl had woken up and seemed disorientated and confused. "What's going on?"

Oliver took a step backwards into the room and spoke on a quiet voice. "You were asleep. I put the jacket over you so you were covered up." He motioned towards the corridor outside. "I thought it might be a good idea in case someone came in."

At that, the two drunk boys stumbled past the doorway, talking loudly and boisterously. The young girl realised that she was in a compromising situation and sat up to try and get her bearings.

"Maybe you should go home." Oliver pulled his phone out of the pocket of his jeans. "Do you want me to call you a taxi?"

The young girl rubbed her face and spoke in a bleary manner. "No thanks. I can walk. I don't live too far from here." She tried to focus on his face. "You're Oliver, aren't you? You're in my history class."

"Yeah, that's right." He pushed his phone back in his pocket. "Diane, isn't it? You sit in front of me."

"Yes, that's me." She stood up uneasily and made her way over to the pile of jackets. "I only came in here to find my coat. I suppose I had better go."

"It's very late. Where do you live?"

Diane named a street not far from Sanctuary Green.

"That's close to me. Can I see you home? It's not a good idea to walk by yourself."

"Thanks, I think my friends might have left already."

The two of them smiled at each other and left the party together. There would be no overburdened consciences or tormenting regrets after this night, just faith in human kindness. Life can be easy if you do the simple things, and nothing is as simple as having respect.

Chapter 11

The four friends had each been tested on the night of the party and they had all passed with the best possible grades. Each of them had scored an A* for self-respect, compassion and forethought. If life was a school then they had learnt the lessons, taken the exams and graduated top of the class. It was now time for them to face the world.

To turn a dark past into a bright future you must bring light to the present. Although they had all turned a corner they were still hurting due to what was happening in their home lives. This could not be solved by hate and anger, but by love and hope. It was time to go back to where it all started.

Leanne stood at the end of the driveway gathering the courage to enter her home. The sight of the house invoked many emotions, but few of them were good ones. For such a long time all it had brought were arguments and ill will that had led to pain and anguish. This had to change.

As Leanne walked through the front door she could hear sounds coming from the kitchen, so she made her way in. She watched, unmoving, while her parents prepared separate meals, unaware of their daughter's presence. They did not speak to each other as they chopped meat and diced carrots. The only time either of them acknowledged the other one's presence was when they got in one another's way, with an exaggerated tut. It was the usual venomous atmosphere that regularly poisoned this family home.

"Could I talk to you both please?" said Leanne.

"Yes, of course."

"OK, go on."

Sarah and Paul did not avert their attention from the task in hand and carried on preparing their food. Although they were now aware of their daughter's presence they still were not giving her their full attention. This was not about to be accepted.

"Could you stop what you're doing and listen to me please." Leanne slightly raised her voice. "I need you to hear everything I'm going to say."

Sarah looked up from chopping her potatoes, while Paul put down the colander full of cauliflower. Now that they were fully focused on their daughter they realised that something was wrong. They could see the sadness in her face and, as a result, a look of concern crossed theirs. It was obvious, even to them, that she had something important to say.

There was no hint of anger in Leanne's voice, but there was certainly pain and sadness. "You two are breaking my heart." Those first words sent a shiver down her spine and she took a moment to get a grip of herself. "Whenever you argue it may not hurt you, but it hurts me terribly. Every time you say the cruel things to each other that you do, I suffer. Those moments when you clearly show that you don't love each other, it's me who feels unloved. I can't go on like this. You two are destroying me."

The remonstrations began immediately.

"We don't do it to hurt you." Sarah put her hands on her hips. "It's got nothing to do with you."

"Nothing we say is aimed at you." Paul crossed his arms. "It's just that parents get angry with each other sometimes."

"Your father annoys me and I get angry."

"Don't blame me!"

"Well, it's not my fault."

"You start the arguments."

"I start the arguments? You keep leaving your sports bag in the hall when I've told you not to do it."

"So move it then. It's not hard. At least I don't spend eighty pounds on a handbag."

"SHUT UP!"

There was a tense silence. All three of them stood there without saying a word. A tear rolled down Leanne's cheek. Sarah came over to try to wipe it away, but her hand was pushed away.

"Leave it. I want you both to see." Leanne looked at each of her parents in turn. "If it wasn't for you two, I wouldn't be crying in the first place. Wiping a tear away doesn't remove the cause."

"But I don't want to see you upset." Sarah pleaded with her daughter. "We only get angry with each other. Not you."

"You don't do anything to annoy us." Paul said in a calm manner. "Mum and Dad get a bit angry with each other when we disagree about things. Parents do that sometimes."

Leanne closed her eyes to gain some composure and then spoke in an imploring manner. "Have you got any idea how terrible it makes me feel when you two argue? The things you say are so spiteful. How can you possibly believe that it won't affect me? How do you think I feel when someone is so nasty to my mum and so insulting to my dad? How do you think it feels when my dad is called a lazy bastard and my mum a useless bitch? I don't want to hear either of you being cruel to each other like that. It might not affect you, but it cuts right through me."

Leanne addressed Sarah. "Mum, when I was ill as a child you would always cuddle me, but who am I meant to go to when it's you who is making me feel so awful?" Her attention turned to Paul. "Dad, when I got hurt, when I was young, you consoled me, but who's going to console me when it's you who is causing the pain? You two may not love each other anymore, and I know there is nothing I can do about that, but please, please, please, show that you care about me enough to at least not hate each other, because I have never felt so much hate in all my life." She began to cry uncontrollably. "And I'm so broken. I can't take it anymore. I just want to feel loved."

Sarah and Paul had tears in their eyes too. For a long moment they stood, frozen to the spot, wracked with guilt. They loved their daughter, but had not realised how much damage their constant arguing was doing to her. In a moment of clarity they had found out they had hurt someone who they were both meant to love from the depths of their hearts, and the realisation made them feel awful.

With remorse and shame, Sarah and Paul went over to Leanne and embraced her. It was a long while since they had been so close to each other as a family. All that mattered to Sarah and Paul, in that moment, was the welfare of their daughter. Their hostilities had been put on hold and the person in their arms was the centre of their attention. It was time to change and they had no choice but to make some heartfelt promises.

"I'm so sorry my darling," said Sarah. "I had no idea." She hugged her daughter tightly. "We'll do our best never to hurt you like that again."

Paul closed his eyes and spoke with a rare sincerity. "I can't believe that I've hurt you so badly. How could we have done such a thing?" He kissed Leanne on the cheek. "We've been fools; utter fools."

For the first time in far too long Sarah and Paul spoke about themselves as a partnership. It had not been a declaration of affection for each other, but a demonstration of love for their wonderful daughter. As the three of them embraced, the past was put to rest so that the future could begin.

From that moment on Sarah and Paul never again had a full-blown argument in front of Leanne. There were times when they said something cutting to each other, but as soon as they saw the hurt in their daughter's eyes, it was enough to get them to stop. Her pain had become their pain. They eventually got into the habit of not having arguments for the sake of it. It was all they had to do.

Leanne's life became a lot better. When she came home in the evenings she was not scared of what she was going to encounter when she walked through the door. All she had to think about was the usual things that a teenager would have on their mind: music, fashion, friends and fun. That was all she wanted. From then on, being able to love others and herself became easy.

Vincent sat in an armchair, staring at the blank television screen. He had no intention of turning it on and waited patiently in solitude. His isolation was welcome as it gave him time to think. Soon he would have company. That would be when it would begin.

It was time for Vincent to confront the problems of his home life. His mother and stepfather needed to hear what he had to say. This would be for his good and theirs. They might not realise it, but in due course they would have no choice but to contemplate their own futures. Things had to be said, lines had to be drawn and decisions had to be made. That was just how it had to be.

When Vincent heard the sound of the front door opening he did not get flustered or nervous. He remained calm and contemplative. This was too important to get wrong. Too much depended on it.

Fiona walked into the living room with Jade in her arms. She seemed anxious and it was not too long before it became apparent what about. Jack followed closely behind, with a pack of four beer cans in his hands and a scowl on his face. He was clearly angry.

"He's lucky I didn't knock him out." Jack made his hand into a fist. "I was ready for him!"

"He was quite big though." Fiona sounded cautious. "I'm glad it didn't kick off."

"I don't care how big he was. He could've killed us the way he was driving. It was my right of way." Jack was shaking so hard with rage that when he opened one of the cans, he spilt beer over his wrist. "I had a tyre iron in the back. I would've used it on him as well."

"I was a bit scared for a moment."

Jack was not about to have his masculinity diminished. "I wasn't scared. I don't care how big he was. I would've done him."

Vincent regarded his stepfather. He had heard these types of conversations before. There had been many times when Jack had got involved in a fracas while out in public. Stories of him shouting and swearing at people were common. They rarely resulted in violence though. Anyone who was the same size or bigger than him was invariably 'let off'.

When Vincent spoke, his words were aimed at both his mother and stepfather. "Do you know what scares me more than anything?" His expression became pensive. "In fact, it terrifies me."

Fiona looked at her son inquisitively. "No. What?"

There was no reply from Jack. In fact, he barely acknowledged Vincent had spoken before going back to his can of beer. He did not care about such things as his stepson's welfare.

"Loneliness," said Vincent. "It scares the hell out of me. It happens to so many people. They go through life treating people badly and having no respect for anyone, and then one day they find themselves all alone, because no one cares about them. The thought that one day I might spend week after week, month after month, year after year, on my own because no one wants to be with me fills me with terror. That's why I want to go through life treating people with respect and without making enemies."

Jack sneered at his stepson. "What are you talking about, you idiot? You've got to stick up for yourself when people give you crap."

Vincent ignored the insult and carried on. "One day I'm going to have a family. I want to have children of my own. And I swear to you I will never hurt them. I will make sure they have nothing but respect for me, so that when I grow old they'll want to spend time with me. People only want to be with people who they like. I'm going to make sure my family love me." He looked directly at his stepfather. "Who's going to visit you when you get old, Jack?"

This did not go down well. It was a clear attack on Jack's authority and his response was predictably heated.

"I don't care whether you walk out this house and never come back." Jack stood up. "Just remember who pays the bills here. If it wasn't for me you wouldn't have a roof over your head. You're an ungrateful bastard!"

At that, Jack stormed out of the room. He had not liked a glimpse of his future. It stood to reason that if he spent his life bullying people, no one would like him, and that would, undoubtedly, result in loneliness. He didn't like his stepson spelling out the stark facts.

Fiona had not said a word up to this point. She had felt safer staying out of it. However, she was worried that the same fate as her husband might apply to her.

"You won't leave me all alone will you, Vincent?" Fiona's asked, with a hurt expression. "I know things haven't always been great around here, but I try my best. It's not easy trying to hold together a family."

"Mum, I wouldn't stop you from seeing your grandchildren. You'll always be welcome at any home of mine, but it won't just be up to me. One day I'll tell my partner and children everything. It will be their choice whether they want to visit you or not."

He pointed to the kitchen where his stepfather had gone. "What do you reckon my family will think of him? Do you think they'll want to come here? If he's willing to hit me, would he be willing to hit my children? You know what he's like, and so will any future partner of mine. I mean, let's face it, he's never going to change."

"I know he's been rough on you, but he's been through hard times. He can't always control his temper," said Fiona. "I'll talk to him."

"Everyone can control their temper, Mum. He wouldn't start swinging punches at someone bigger than him. He picks on us because he knows he can get away with it. He doesn't lose control; he lets it go." Vincent leant forward and held his mother's hand. "I don't want you to be lonely, Mum, but I can't make any promises. How will I be able to persuade my family to come here if all they're going to experience is anger and possibly violence? Can you guarantee that he won't be throwing things around or smashing things up in front of my children?"

"No, I suppose I can't," said Fiona eventually. "I wouldn't want your children to see that either." She looked at her son. "You're a good person, Vincent. You'll make a great father one day."

"And you'll make a great grandmother, Mum."

"I hope so."

Two months later, Fiona moved out, taking her two children with her. She rented a place on the other side of town, and they started a new life. The thought of rarely seeing her family had been enough for her to make a change. No one wants to be abandoned and unloved.

Jack had, at first, made a few threats over the phone, but a visit from the police soon put a stop to that. It did not take long for him to lose interest in his daughter either. As usual, he blamed everyone except himself, which gave him some comfort, but that was temporary and did not last long. When it finally sank in that he was all alone it was too late. Karma has a lot of patience and it never forgets.

Things became far less complicated for Vincent after that. A life without violence meant that he had less to be angry about. It took some time to completely clear his mind of the past, but it got a lot easier as the years went by. Pain goes away a lot quicker when the cause of it is no longer present.

As the car pulled up to the kerb one of the back-passenger doors opened and an occupant got out. They immediately walked up the garden path and opened the front door with a key. Once they were inside they headed straight for the living room. The people they wanted to see were always there at this time of day.

Oliver forced a sorrowful smile on his face. His mother frowned at him inquisitively. He then turned to his tormentor. As he spoke his voice was emotional, but resolute. "You must've known that this time would come. You couldn't get away with it forever."

Brian looked up from the book he was reading. He gazed at Oliver in confusion. He had no idea what was going on, but he was sure there would be a rational explanation.

Oliver put his palm on the centre of his chest. "You've broken my heart, you've abused my flesh and you've destroyed your son." There was fury, agony and conviction in his voice. "You did everything possible to devastate my life, but I will not let you get away with ruining it for one day more."

Brian's expression became deeply concerned. What had just been said made him feel intensely uncomfortable. He was not sure what was happening, but when the police officers walked into the room behind his son it all became very apparent.

Jean was also aware that something serious was going on. She sat up in her armchair with a worried look on her face. A woman police officer made her way over to her and beckoned her to join her in the kitchen.

"Jean isn't it? We'd like to have a word with you in private, if that's OK?" the officer said.

"What's this all about?" she turned to her husband. "What have you done?"

Brian motioned to his wife that she should leave. He didn't want her to hear what he suspected was coming next. Although she was reluctant, Jean left the room with the officer.

There were now two uniformed male officers in the living room and one plain-clothed. Brian stared at them both in horror. It was like his soul had been wrenched from his body and left an empty shell of bones and flesh. His blood felt like ice in his veins.

The plain-clothed officer said. "You know why we're here. I suggest you don't say anything until we get to the station. You will need a lawyer." He motioned with his hand at the two uniformed officers. "Cuff him and get him to the car."

Brian tried to talk, but no words came out. The two officers grabbed his wrists and put them behind his back. Within seconds the handcuffs were on and he was being led away while having his rights reads to him. As he was leaving he glanced back at his son who stared after him with hatred and contempt.

"You will never hurt me again," said Oliver. Those were the last words he ever spoke to his father.

At that, Brian was ushered out of the house. That would be the last time he would set foot in the place he called home. He would never be a part of that family again either.

The plain-clothed officer came to stand by Oliver. "You did very well," he said. "That was an extremely hard thing to do. There's no telling how many more victims there could have been in the future if you had not had the courage to speak out. You've saved a lot of people from misery. I have nothing but admiration for you."

A scream came from the kitchen as Jean learnt the excruciating truth. Without hesitation, Oliver immediately rushed to be by his mother's side.

Oliver and his mother did their best to heal the deep wounds that were opened on that day. In an attempt to wipe away the past they moved to a small house nearer the centre of town. It would take many years, but they would do their best to get through it together. Although the scars would always be there, their love would be as well, and that would prove to be a very efficient healer.

Brian pleaded guilty to all of the charges that were levied against him. He had no choice. Oliver had hidden his phone in his bedroom and secretly filmed his father carrying out the acts he was accused of. It all came down to the decision of the judge. Unfortunately, hell is not a place on earth, but prison was the next best thing.

Oliver received counselling to help him confront the reality of what he had gone through. The basis of his treatment was to get him to understand that what he had endured was in no way not normal, so armed with that knowledge, he could strive to become normal. Eventually, he would get the ordinary life he always wanted. Sometimes, enough is more than enough.

The living room was empty, the kitchen was as well. No one was in either of the bedrooms either. Nothing stirred in this cold, empty residence as the usual occupants were elsewhere. A house cannot be a home without a family.

Emma stood on the pavement outside. She had never been in a bar before and felt slightly nervous about entering. Of course, she was underage, but that would not stop her today. It was time for her to take control of her life.

As the door opened the handful of customers inside looked around to see who had entered the bar. They were surprised to see a schoolgirl standing there. Emma saw her mother across the bar, cleaning glasses. She walked straight over to her and stood there without saying a word. When Karen realised that the customer who had just strolled in was actually her daughter she was, understandably, taken aback.

"What are you doing here? You know you're not allowed in here, Emma." Karen put down the glass and made her way around the bar. "You've got to leave, or we'll get in trouble."

"I need to speak to you, Mum." Emma's expression was anxious. "It's really important and it can't wait."

Karen could see that something was seriously amiss. Her daughter was standing in front of her asking for her time. Her instincts as a mother took over. She called out to another member of the staff to ask them to cover for her and then led Emma to the office out the back.

"What's wrong?" Karen motioned towards two chairs by a desk and then sat down. "Are you OK? You're not in trouble are you?"

Emma sat on the edge of the seat and looked at her mother through sad eyes. It would be hard to say everything that she wanted to, but she had prepared long enough for this moment to be able to get her message across. She would have to be direct and forthright, but considerate.

"Mum, I've got problems; really bad problems," said Emma. "I'm suffering from mental health illnesses that are absolutely devastating me. I see things that aren't there and I can't stop my brain from doing things that I don't want it to do. I'm not in control of my own mind. I need help."

"I never knew this." Karen was clearly shocked. "Why didn't you tell me?"

"I never see you, Mum." Emma did not want to put blame where it did not belong, but she also did not want to ignore the causes. "You're always at work. We so rarely spend any time together. I've had no one to talk to about it."

"I have to go to work, Emma. We've got to pay the bills. I don't know what else I can do. We have to be able to afford to live." Karen suddenly realised that she was making excuses. "I'm sorry. It's just so hard. So what is it that's wrong with you? Tell me what the matter is so we can do something about it."

Emma steadied herself and then went about trying to give the best possible explanation. "It's called psychosis, but I call it 'mind lies'. I see things that aren't there; spiders mainly. Sometimes I don't know what's real and what isn't. I also suffer from OCD. I call that 'brain chores'. It makes me do things over and over in my brain even though I don't need to or want to. I have no control over it. It's awful, Mum. It's making me lose my mind."

Karen felt a wave of grief wash over her. "I'm so sorry that I haven't been there for you, Emma. I've been so busy trying to pay the bills and put food on the table that I forgot about you. I never meant for us to drift apart." She realised it was time to help her daughter. "You're all that matters to me. Nothing is more important to me than you. Whatever it takes, we'll find a way through this."

Emma spoke in a confident voice. "I know we will, Mum. We can sort this out." A smile crossed her face. "And I think I have a solution."

"What's that?"

"You know that restaurant where we go sometimes for birthdays and special occasions, why don't you apply for a job there, they always need experienced staff. I'll see if

I can get a job in the kitchen or waiting tables." Emma took hold of her mother's hands. "That we can see more of each other and I can help you to pay the bills, so you won't have to do so many hours. We could even save up and have a short break away together. It will fun."

"Well," said Karen. "Maybe it could work, we can certainly try. We'll apply together. With the extra money we'll make sure we go on that holiday. As for your mental health problems," she said in a determined voice. "We'll make an appointment to see someone as quickly as possible. We'll look into it and find the best help for you. You and I will fight this together. Whatever you go through, I go through."

"It will be you and me, Mum." Emma's eyes were filled with tears. "You and me."

They hugged each other harder than ever before.

From that point on, Emma and Karen became a really close team. They did so much with each other. Shifts worked, meals eaten and holidays taken. An inseparable bond was formed that would see them continue to be close for the rest of their lives. It was an alliance built out of an indestructible material called love.

Karen found a counsellor for Emma and she attended the sessions regularly. Her progress was both steady and constant. Emma came to accept her mental health problems as being a part of who she was, and learnt coping mechanisms. What she could not control, she learnt to live with. Sometimes a battle within can be ended by negotiating a truce.

Chapter 12

Many years passed and many good decisions had been made. The lessons of the past had been learnt, actions had been taken and hope lit the way for a bright future. There were no more perpetrators or victims, just calm minds and content souls. Happiness was infectious and it spread to all who desired it.

Two decades on from those days at school, the four friends met in their usual place in the park where they had always gone to catch up with each other. Stories of yesteryear were swapped and memories exchanged fondly. The sad stories that could have been spoken of were left untold. Only the good times were mentioned on this fine day.

The four of them lay on the grass in the shape of a cross, with their heads adjacent to each other, looking up at bright sky. Next to each of them was their respective partners while those who had children let them play in amongst them.

Leanne lay there contemplating what had come to be. Throughout her life she had been approached by men who had wanted to make her their next boast. Every one of them had all been turned away with ease. No one treated her disrespectfully; they would not dare. When it came to looking for a partner only those with honesty and morality had even been considered. If love is a finely cut diamond, never pick up a rough piece of coal.

Leanne's life had obviously not been perfect. She had experienced some unsuccessful relationships. At one point she had even been engaged to a man who she had dated for two years, but they had mutually broken it off when they realised they had both changed who they were and what they wanted. An important part of life is to accept that change is inevitable and make sure that, when it happens, it is for the better. There is never any shame in admitting that you have got something wrong. The worst mistakes are the ones that are not recognised.

Lying next to Leanne was her husband, Dean. They had met one autumn when neither of them had been intentionally looking for a partner. Chance had meant they had crossed paths and magnetism had guided them together. Their first date had ended with a solitary kiss. It took a lot more nights out after that before physical contact occurred. There was no doubt in either of their minds that each other's feelings were of a paramount importance. This is how it was and how it would always be. The best relationships start slowly, so that they do not finish quickly.

Marriage had been the next step when they were both sure that their future was meant to be spent together. It was not a decision that had been rushed. A son and daughter had been brought into the world in the following years. Never was there a happier family. Not once did their children witness anger exchanged between their parents; only love and affection. They would grow up to pass on what they had learnt. People only give out what they are given in the first place.

Leanne was extremely happy in life. She deserved to be. Every time that she had needed to make the right decision she had done so. In the end doing the right thing had become effortless. When it comes to self-respect, it grows with making the right choices.

Oliver let his mind wander as he lay there. What he had been through and the scars that he carried would live with him forever, but at least the cause of it was no longer in his life. His father spent a lot of years in prison for what he had done. Not even his name was mentioned again by those who were once his family. No one knew what became of him after he was released, because no one cared.

Life had been extremely hard for Oliver for a number of years after the dust had settled, but he always had the support that he needed close by. His mother had helped him get through the hardship that he had been exposed to and he had done likewise for her. They had both been deeply affected by the events that had passed, but they had drawn strength from each other and forged a resilience that would never weaken. There was, however, another who was a part of his life. If hearts hold love, the biggest ones have the most to give.

Since Oliver had walked Diane home from the party they had spent a lot of time together. It had not been easy for him to get close to another person and he needed understanding more than anything else. Diane knew that not everything was right with this young man whom she had grown to love, but she was willing to wait for him to be ready. There were times when he could not be touched, so she withdrew just far enough away so that she was still in reach. On other occasions, she needed to be as close as possible, so she held him in her arms so that he felt safe. He could not have asked for a more sympathetic and considerate person to lean on and fall in love with. The tallest mountains have the highest ridges at their sides.

Oliver's life was uncomplicated. He enjoyed simple things like going to the shops and buying groceries. Queuing in the bank was never a chore. As for going for walks in the countryside, that was a joy. Average was great, but family life was fantastic. Sometimes, ordinary is all that is needed.

His two boys and a girl were Oliver's pride and joy. They were his princes and princess. He gave them one of the most valuable gifts any child could wish for: the warmth of a father's love, and that alone made them rich beyond their wildest dreams. In return he only ever saw adoration in their eyes, and that was utterly priceless. Children are the most truthful mirrors that a parent can look into.

Oliver had got the normal life that he craved simply because he made sure he did not become a reflection of what he had suffered. He may have gone through hell, but he made sure that those around him only knew heaven. His family provided him with a wellspring of love that would never run dry and that was all he had hoped for.

Vincent pondered the life that he had led. He had been forced to carry someone else's anger when he was young, but he had shed that load when he realised that he did not have to bear that burden. Just because something is passed on to someone it does not mean they have to take it. It is pointless to suffer torment, especially if it belongs to someone else.

As Vincent reached adulthood he realised that his life would be better if he lived to his strengths. He was a muscular man and such a physique would be wasted in a career that would not utilise it. When he joined the police he wore the uniform with great pride. Levelheaded and fair, he was an exceptional officer who was highly regarded amongst his peers. In fact, his patrol partner had nothing but respect for him, and that was essential in such a dangerous profession. If you are going to stand on the edge of a cliff, you need to make sure the person behind you is a friend.

Vincent and Josh had joined the force together. After completing their probation it was an obvious decision to put them together. When a violent criminal needed to be apprehended they always had each other's back. If someone needed to be pulled from a burning car they did it together. When an old lady was lost they gave her a lift home. They were a great team and there was not a situation that the two of them could not deal with. If you have great friends, it does not matter who your enemies are.

There was an occasion when the two police officers had been called to diffuse a fight that had broken out in a bar. They had got there just as it was coming to an end. It quickly became apparent who it centred around. Jack, Vincent's ex-stepfather was in the middle of the pub with his fists raised and in an intense rage. However, as he saw his former stepson in full uniform approach, his face went gaunt and his shoulders slumped. No more punches were thrown that day. He gave himself up quietly and passively, with the utter humiliation of knowing that the boy he had once bullied had become the man he could never be.

Vincent lived a fulfilled life, but he had never felt such pride as when his wife, Chloe, gave birth to their son. He had never held a living being as lovingly as he had that boy. There was no shame when the tears fell from his cheeks on to his newborn baby's head.

Fiona absolutely adored her grandson. She visited as much as she could and she always looked forward to the occasions when the special people in her life came to see her. The days of anger and violence were long gone, replaced by only warmth and fondness. Her decision to choose real love was the best she had made. There is never a better investment than family.

At no point would Vincent's son see anger in his father's eyes. If he did something naughty he would only see disappointment on his father's face and that would be enough to make him regret it. As he grew up he would look up to the man he called 'Dad' with admiration and affection. There are many lessons to be learnt in life and the most important ones can only be taught by a caring role model. Being able to love is the best skill a person can acquire.

Vincent was a proud father and loving husband. His family only knew happiness. They were devoted to him, because he adored them, but that was only possible because he had learnt to care about himself. Love can only be passed on if it is owned in the first place.

Emma cleared her mind of all thoughts, as she had trained herself to do. Her mental health problems had never completely disappeared, but at least she now had a certain degree of control over them. If her 'mind lies' made her see spiders she treated them as though they were nothing more than annoying flies and waited patiently for them to go away, with little stress. When her 'brain chores' became too much and gave her numbers to add up or shapes to make symmetrical she would put all the coins from one part of her purse into another, therefore giving herself another pointless task that was more favourable than the previous one. Quite simply, she had taken ownership of her consciousness and had decided what went on inside her own head. Unwanted thoughts are like unwelcome guests at a party; if they were not invited send them away.

Emma never had to get off drugs, because she never tried them in the first place. She did, however, take up the battle against them. After she obtained a psychology degree at university she acquired a government grant and opened up her own counselling clinic for people with mental health illnesses, whether caused by drugs or not. By simplifying the approach to providing therapy for the mind she made it easy to grasp and accessible to all. Sometimes life is complicated because people do not try the easy option first.

Emma wrote a book about modernising mental health definitions so that everyone could understand every type of illness. It sold well enough to bring her quite a lot of attention and she made a few appearances on television to speak about it. After lobbying politicians, she got the government to change its health policies so that remedies for illnesses of the mind became as readily available as they were for accidental cuts and broken bones. The brain is always the first part of the body to feel pain, so it should never be the last to be treated.

It was not long before Emma's business started to expand so she needed to find someone suitable to help her to run it. Since she had met Kim Warnock at the party and discovered that they had so much in common they had been inseparable, but her close friend had found herself in an unrewarding office job. Emma, therefore, talked her into attaining a diploma in counselling and paid for the course. The two of them procured a city council contract to visit surrounding schools to teach pupils how to communicate with their friends about mental health. Their philosophy was simple. If a child knows how to put on a plaster they should know how to listen.

Emma met her partner, Kelly, while on holiday overseas. It had been a long distant relationship at first, but after a year they moved in together. There had never been any talk of marriage, but when a couple consists of a psychologist and a lawyer their careers tend to take centre stage. They loved one another and that was enough. Not everyone's journey in life has the same destination, but happiness is a large place with room for all.

Emma had flown free from the prison of her mind. Soaring high herself was not enough though. Her real pleasure was brought about by mending the broken wings of others. If the goal of life is to gain happiness, then the best way to get it is to bestow it on others.

So that was how things came to be for the four friends. They had all made the decision to take control of their own destinies and not let others choose their journeys for them. Learning to love themselves and those around them had been the most important lesson they had learnt in life. There was no big secret to their success. In fact, it was relatively uncomplicated. It had all come down to them answering that one question they had been asked all those years ago. So now it is your turn.

"Who will live your life?"